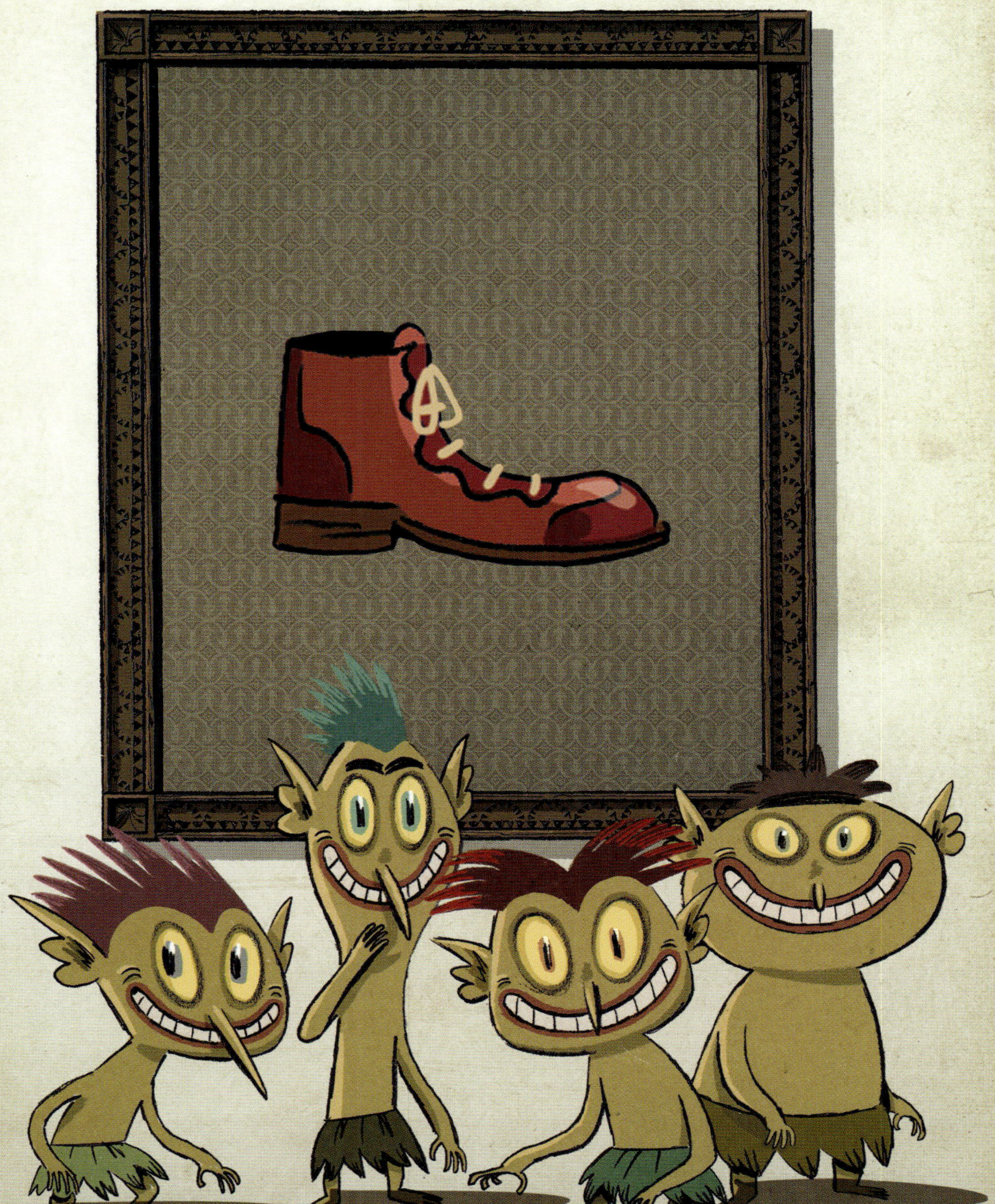

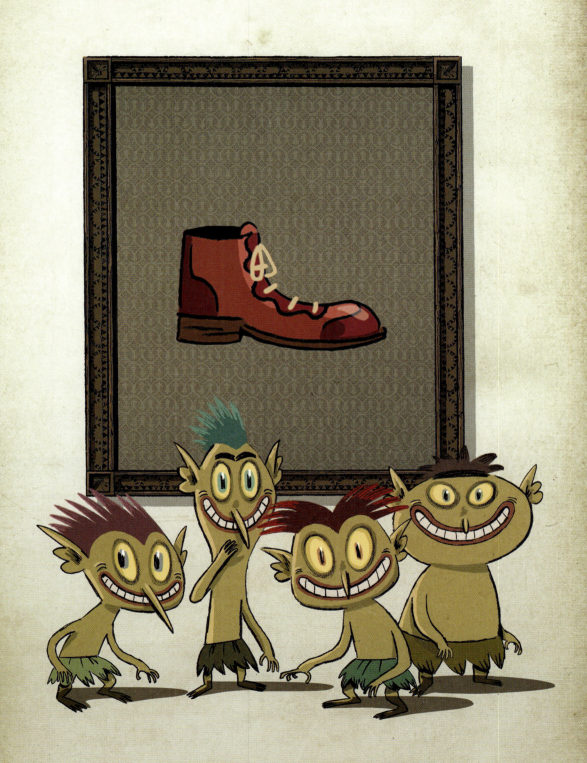

Graphic Spin is published by Stone Arch Books
A Capstone Imprint
151 Good Counsel Drive, P.O. Box 669
Mankato, Minnesota 56002
www.capstonepub.com

Library of Congress Cataloging-in-Publication Data
Powell, Martin.
The elves and the shoemaker : a Grimm graphic novel / retold by Martin Powell ; illustrated by Pedro Rodriquez.
p. cm. -- (Graphic spin)
ISBN 978-1-4342-2553-5 (library binding)
1. Graphic novels. [1. Graphic novels. 2. Fairy tales. 3. Folklore--Germany.] I. Rodríquez, Pedro, ill. II. Grimm, Jacob, 1785-1863. III. Grimm, Wilhelm, 1786-1859. IV. Elves and the shoemaker. English. V. Title.
PZ7.7.P69El 2011
741.5'973--dc22
2010025335

Graphic Designer: Hilary Wacholz | Art Director: Kay Fraser

Summary: Emrick the shoemaker can barely afford food for himself and his wife, but they still give far more than they take. One day, Emrick's generosity compels him to trade a pair of his shoes for a beautiful woodlands painting. He hangs the curious work of art on the wall and goes to sleep hungry. The next morning, he awakens to find a beautifully-crafted pair of shoes resting upon his desk. Later that night, Emrick and his wife watch from the shadows as several tiny elves emerge from inside the magical painting!

Printed in the United States of America in North Mankato, Minnesota.
092010
005933CGS11

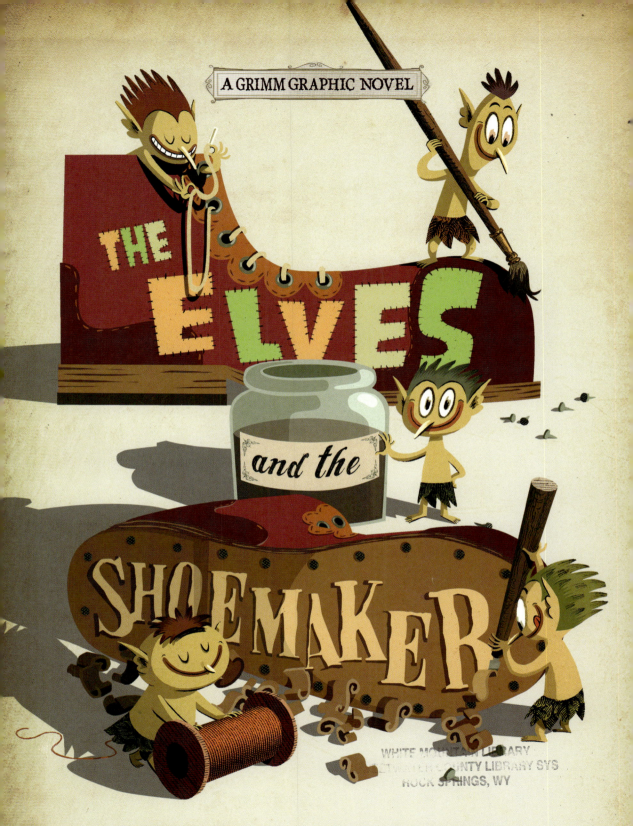

A GRIMM GRAPHIC NOVEL

THE ELVES

and the

SHOEMAKER

retold by Martin Powell   illustrated by Pedro Rodriguez

STONE ARCH BOOKS
a capstone imprint

Cast of Characters

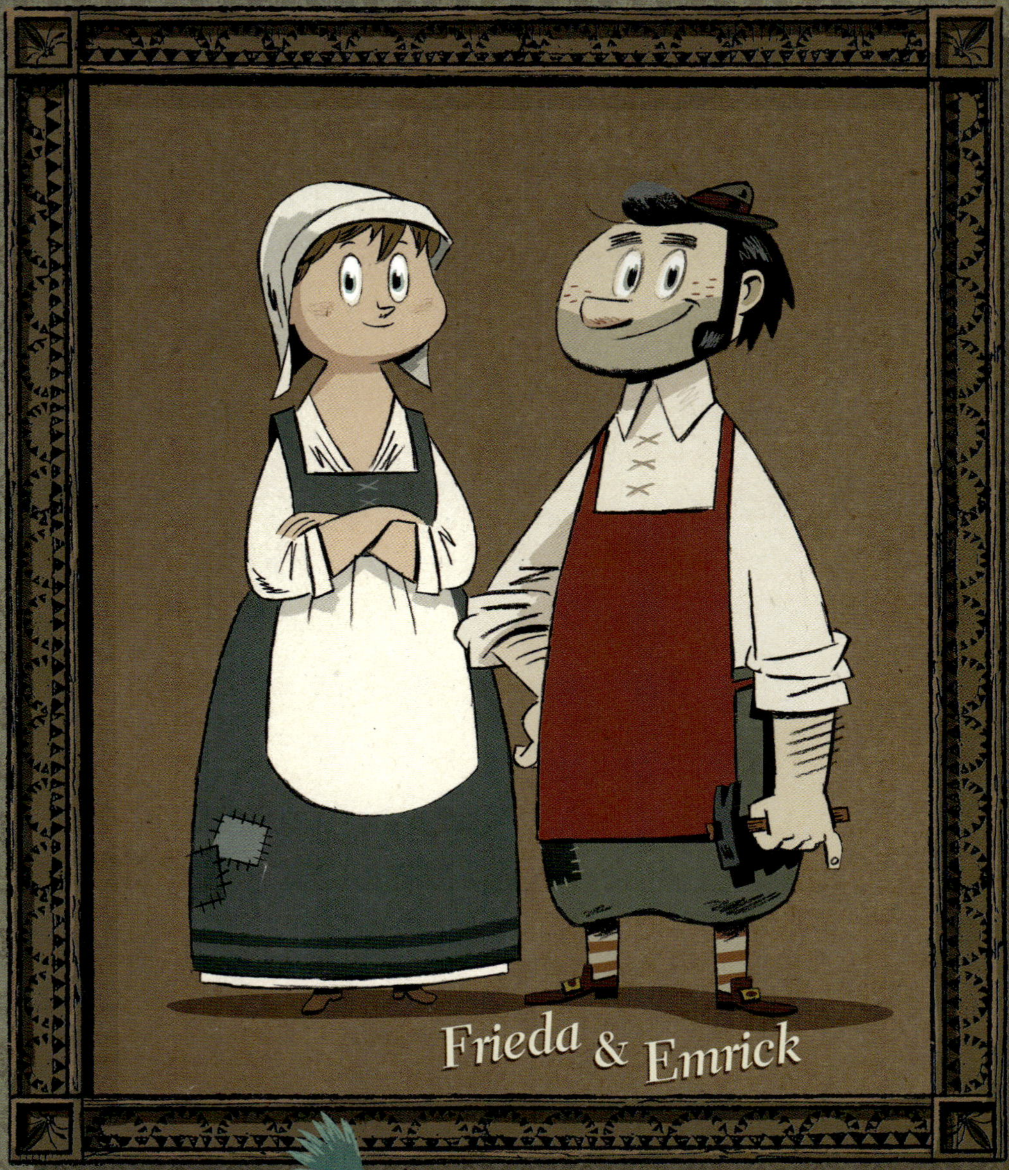
Frieda & Emrick

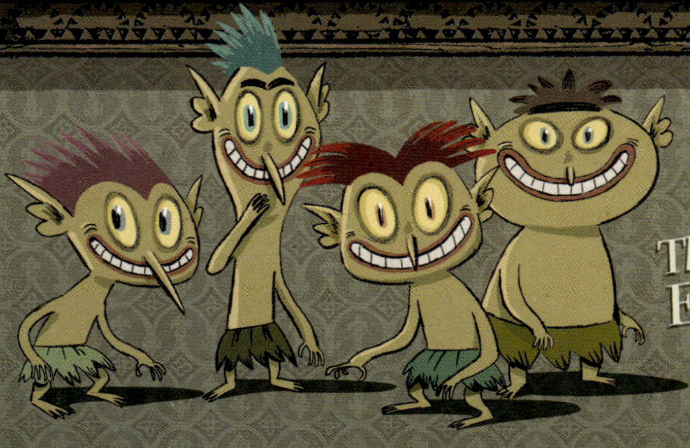
The Elves

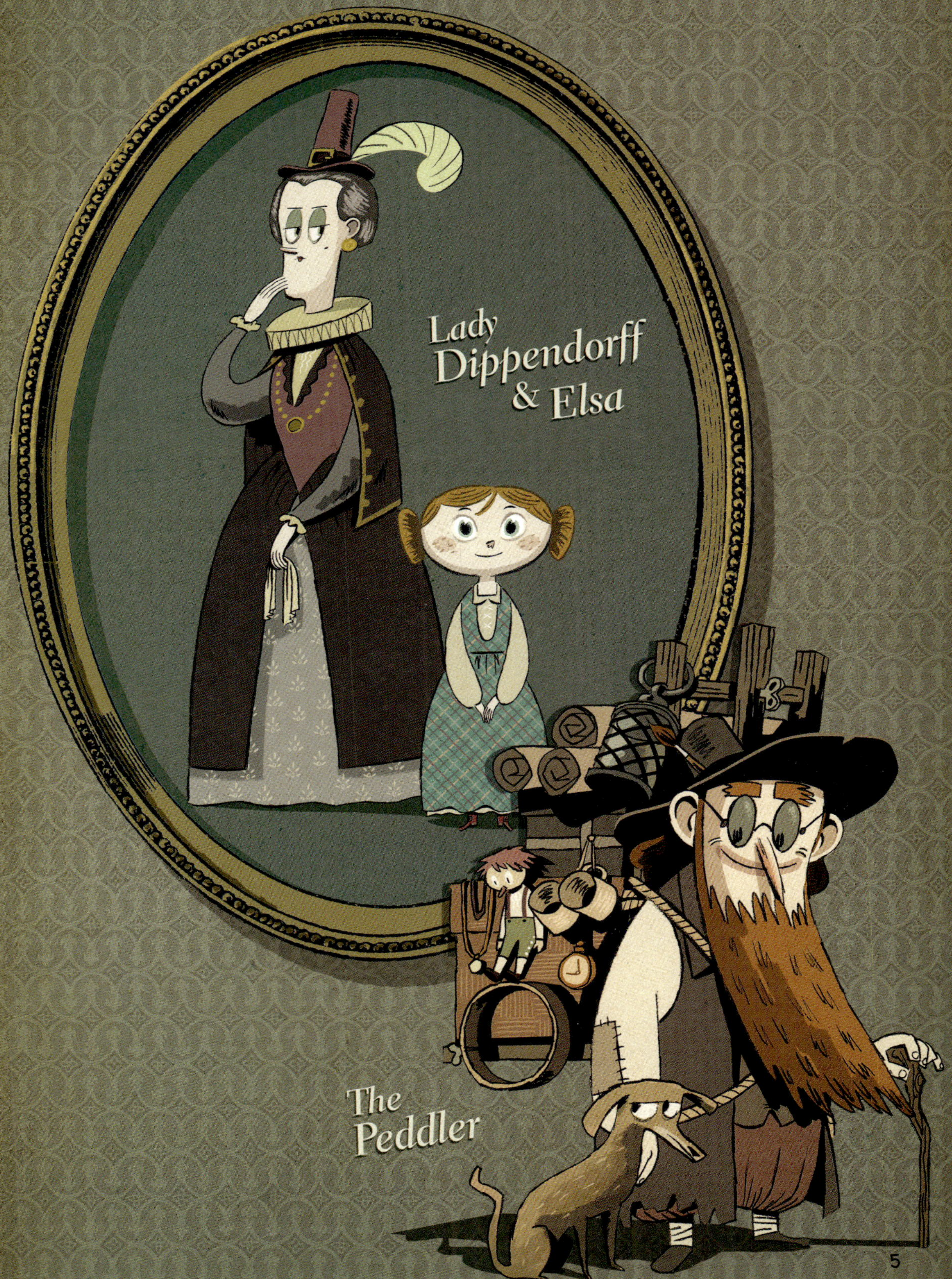
Lady Dippendorff & Elsa
The Peddler

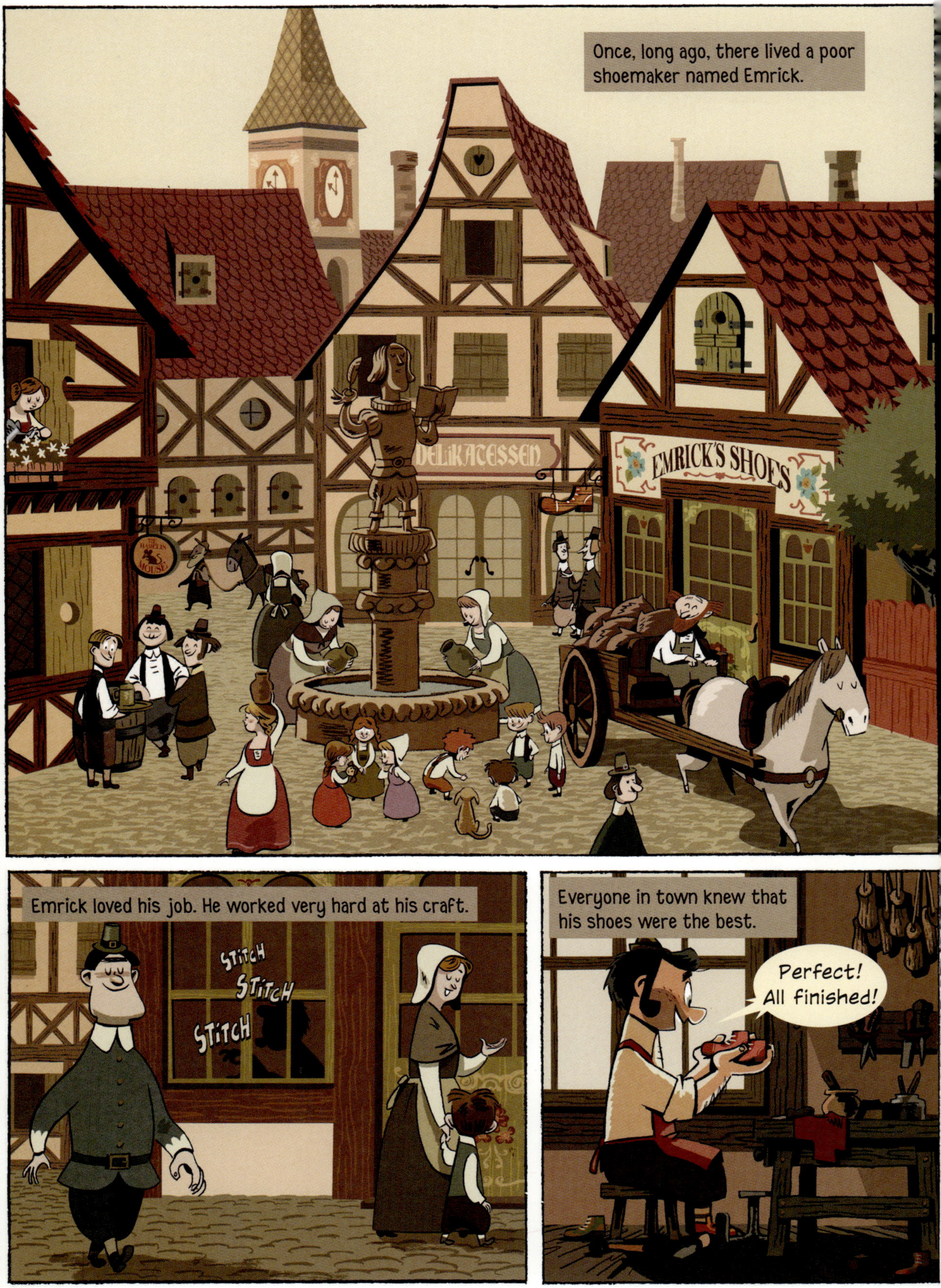
Once, long ago, there lived a poor shoemaker named Emrick.
DELIKATESSEN
EMRICK'S SHOES
Emrick loved his job. He worked very hard at his craft.
STITCH
STITCH
STITCH
Everyone in town knew that his shoes were the best.
Perfect! All finished!

The shoemaker might not have been the richest man in town . . .

Hi there, kids!

. . . but he was very kind.

People throughout the land knew of Emrick's generosity.

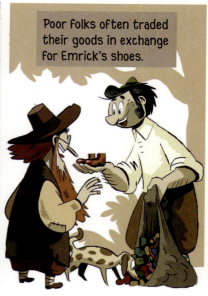

Poor folks often traded their goods in exchange for Emrick's shoes.

That suited him just fine.

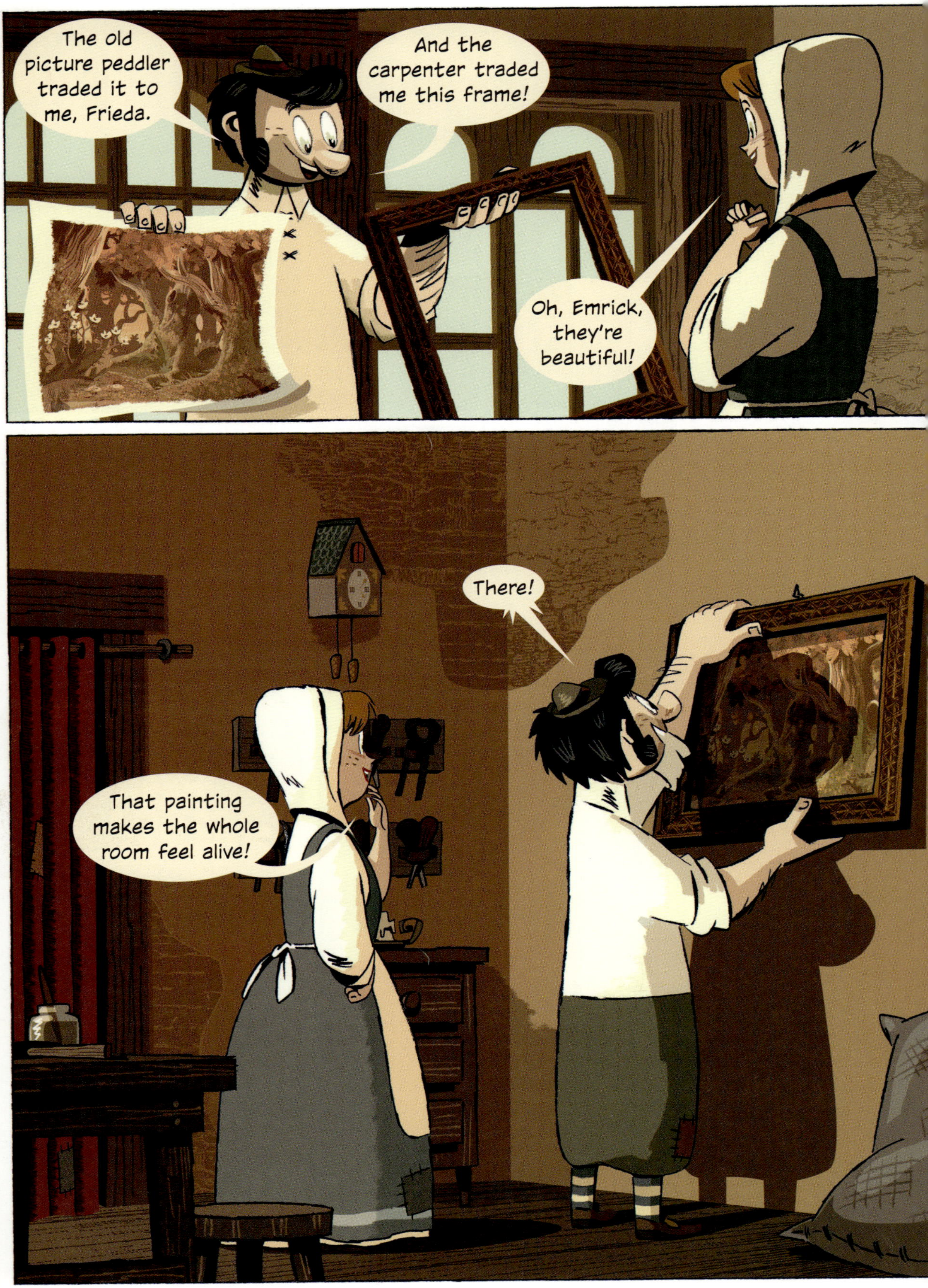

The old picture peddler traded it to me, Frieda.
And the carpenter traded me this frame!
Oh, Emrick, they're beautiful!
There!
That painting makes the whole room feel alive!

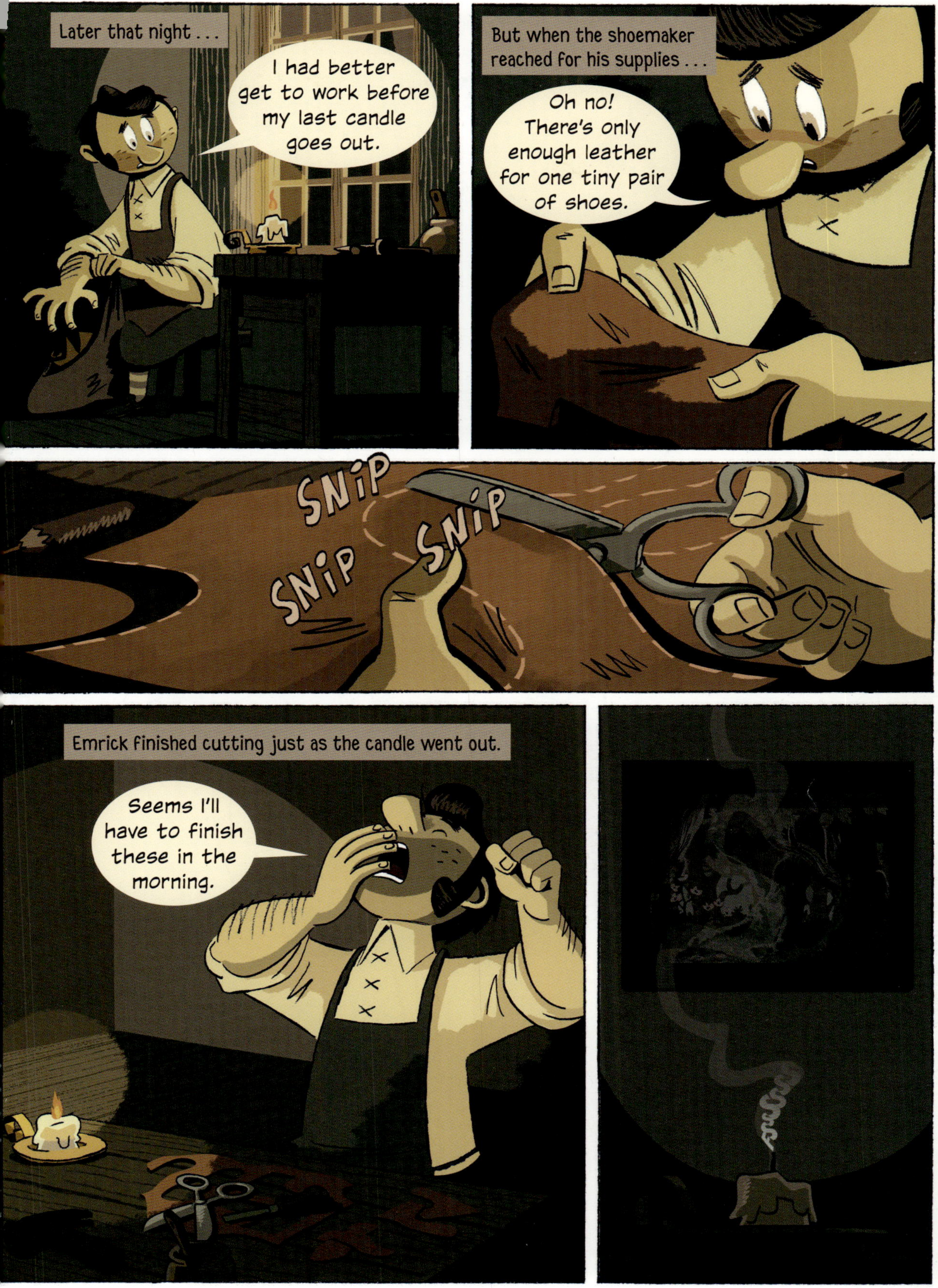
Later that night . . .
I had better get to work before my last candle goes out.
But when the shoemaker reached for his supplies . . .
Oh no! There's only enough leather for one tiny pair of shoes.
SNIP
SNIP
SNIP
Emrick finished cutting just as the candle went out.
Seems I'll have to finish these in the morning.

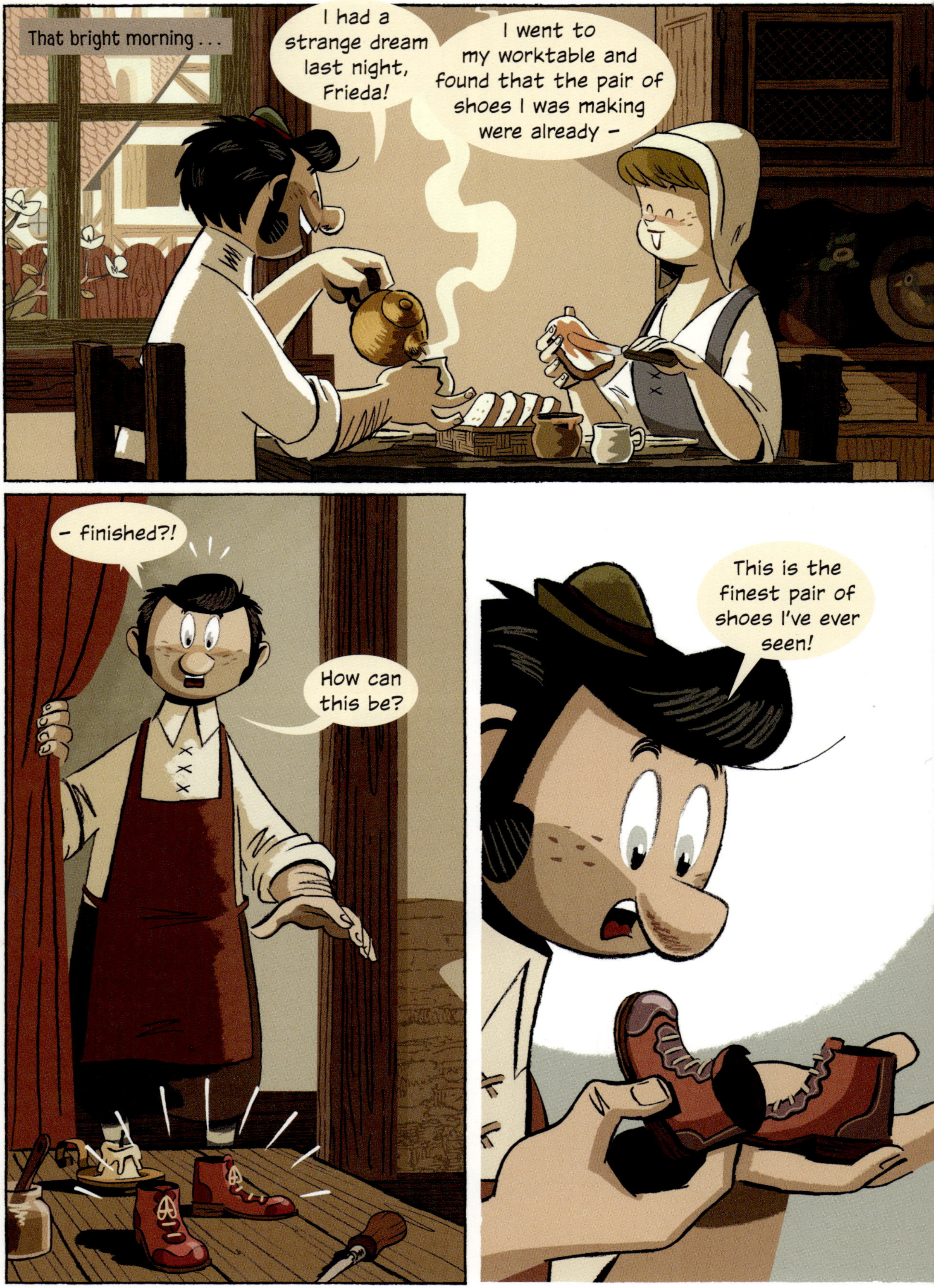
That bright morning . . .
I had a strange dream last night, Frieda!
I went to my worktable and found that the pair of shoes I was making were already –
– finished?!
How can this be?
This is the finest pair of shoes I've ever seen!

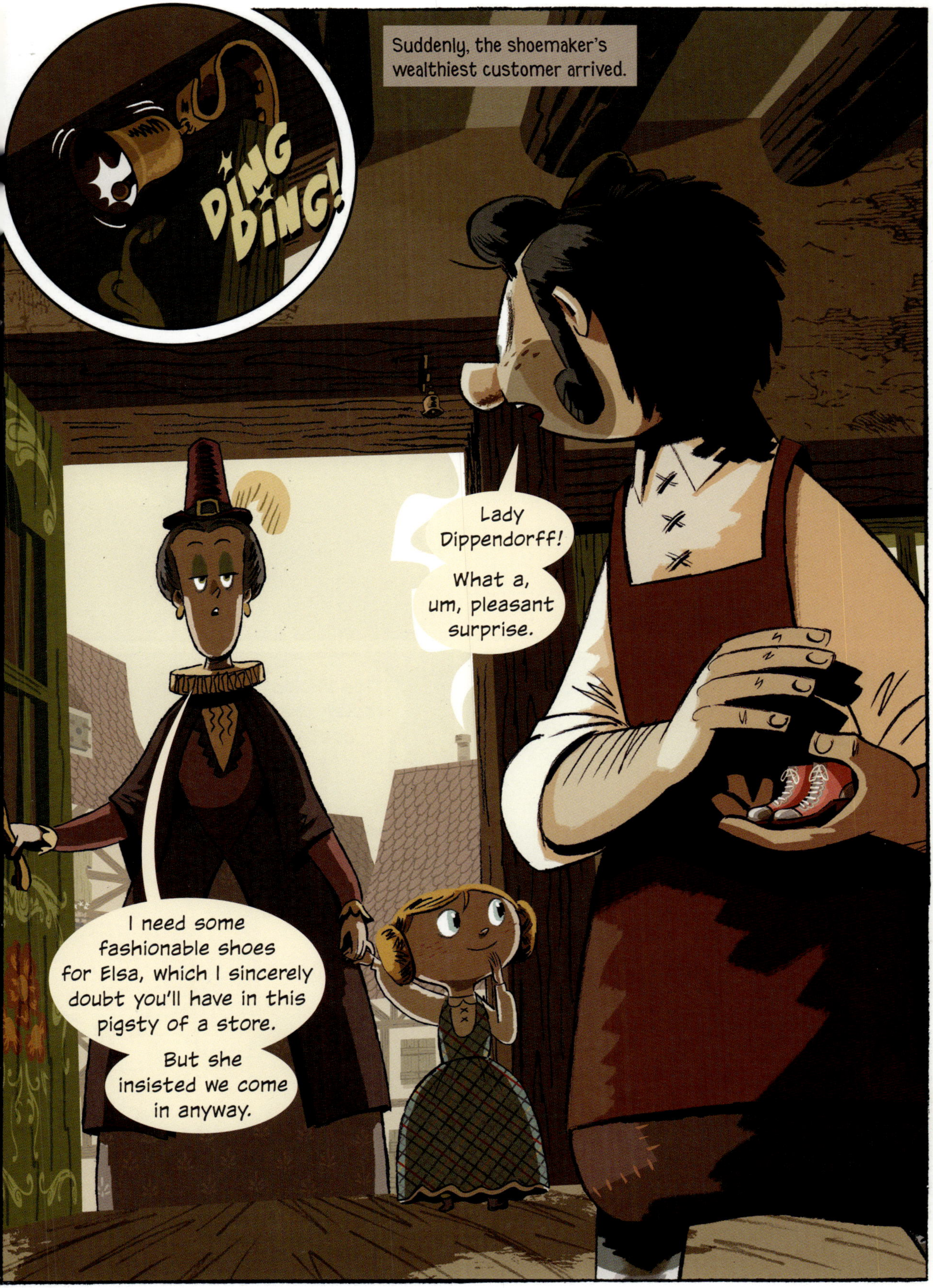
DING DING!
Suddenly, the shoemaker's wealthiest customer arrived.
Lady Dippendorff!
What a, um, pleasant surprise.
I need some fashionable shoes for Elsa, which I sincerely doubt you'll have in this pigsty of a store.
But she insisted we come in anyway.

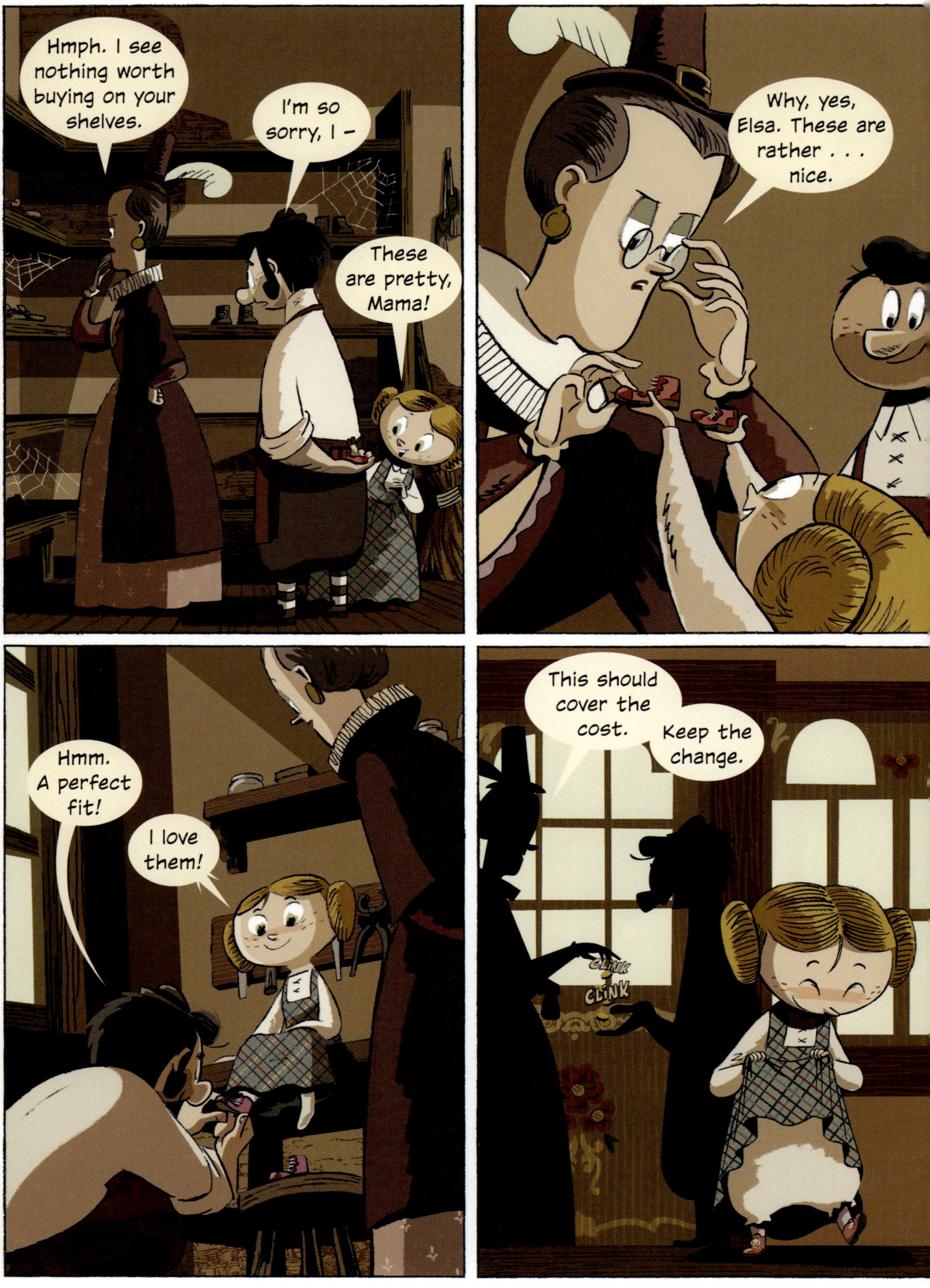
Hmph. I see nothing worth buying on your shelves.
I'm so sorry, I –
These are pretty, Mama!
Why, yes, Elsa. These are rather . . . nice.
Hmm. A perfect fit!
I love them!
This should cover the cost.
Keep the change.
CLINK
CLINK

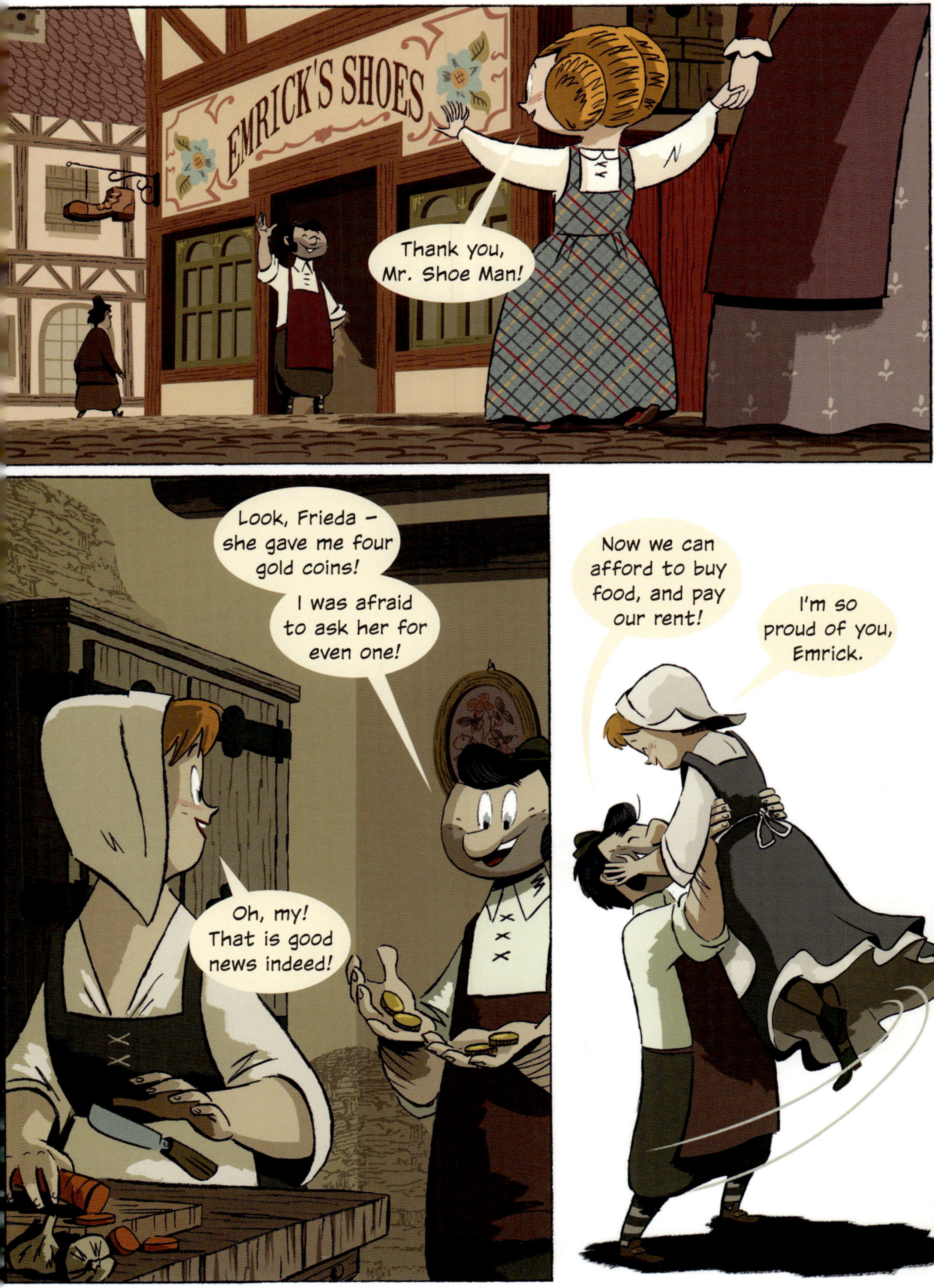
EMRICK'S SHOES
Thank you, Mr. Shoe Man!
Look, Frieda - she gave me four gold coins!
I was afraid to ask her for even one!
Oh, my! That is good news indeed!
Now we can afford to buy food, and pay our rent!
I'm so proud of you, Emrick.

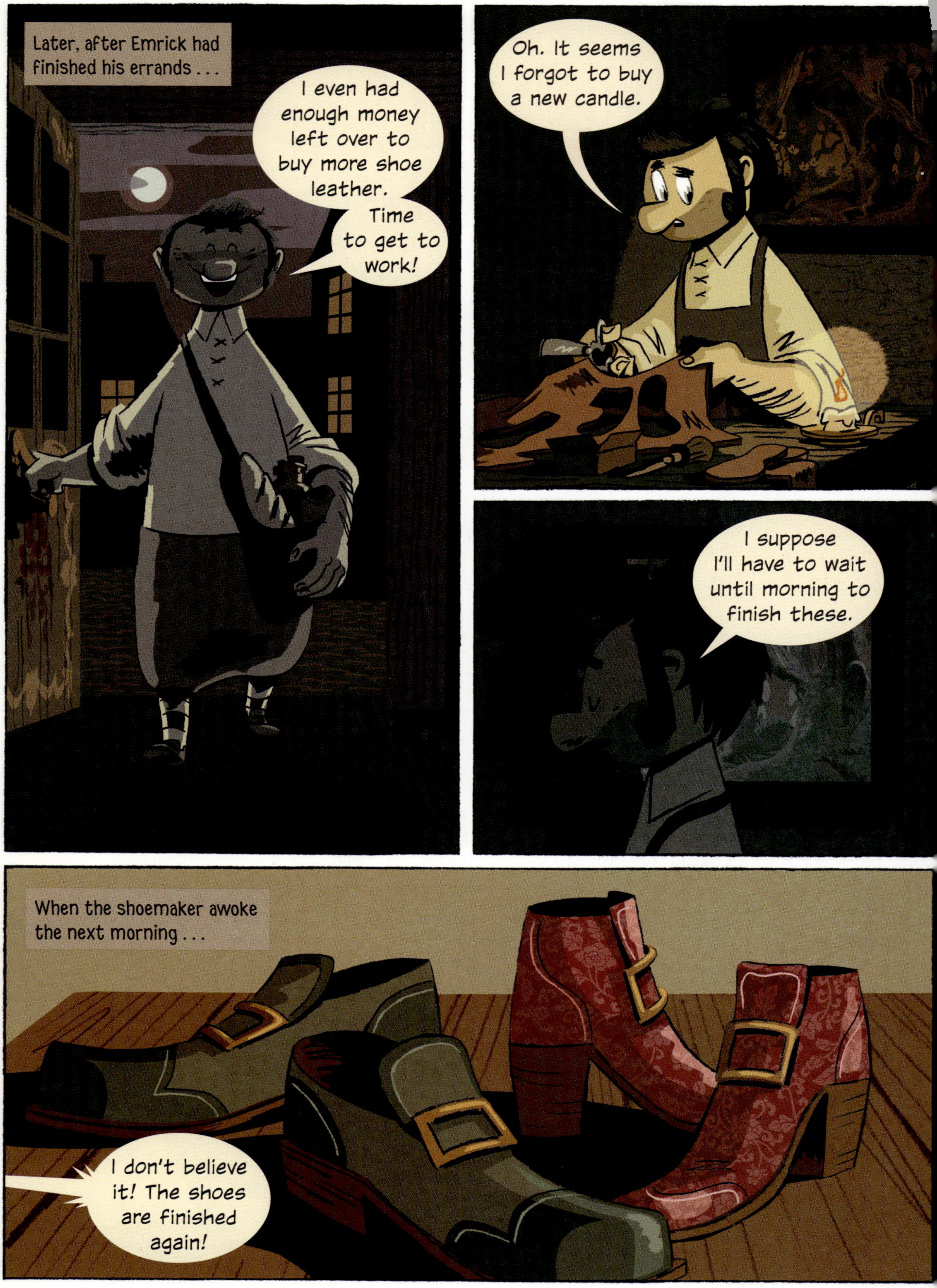
Later, after Emrick had finished his errands . . .
I even had enough money left over to buy more shoe leather.
Time to get to work!
Oh. It seems I forgot to buy a new candle.
I suppose I'll have to wait until morning to finish these.
When the shoemaker awoke the next morning . . .
I don't believe it! The shoes are finished again!

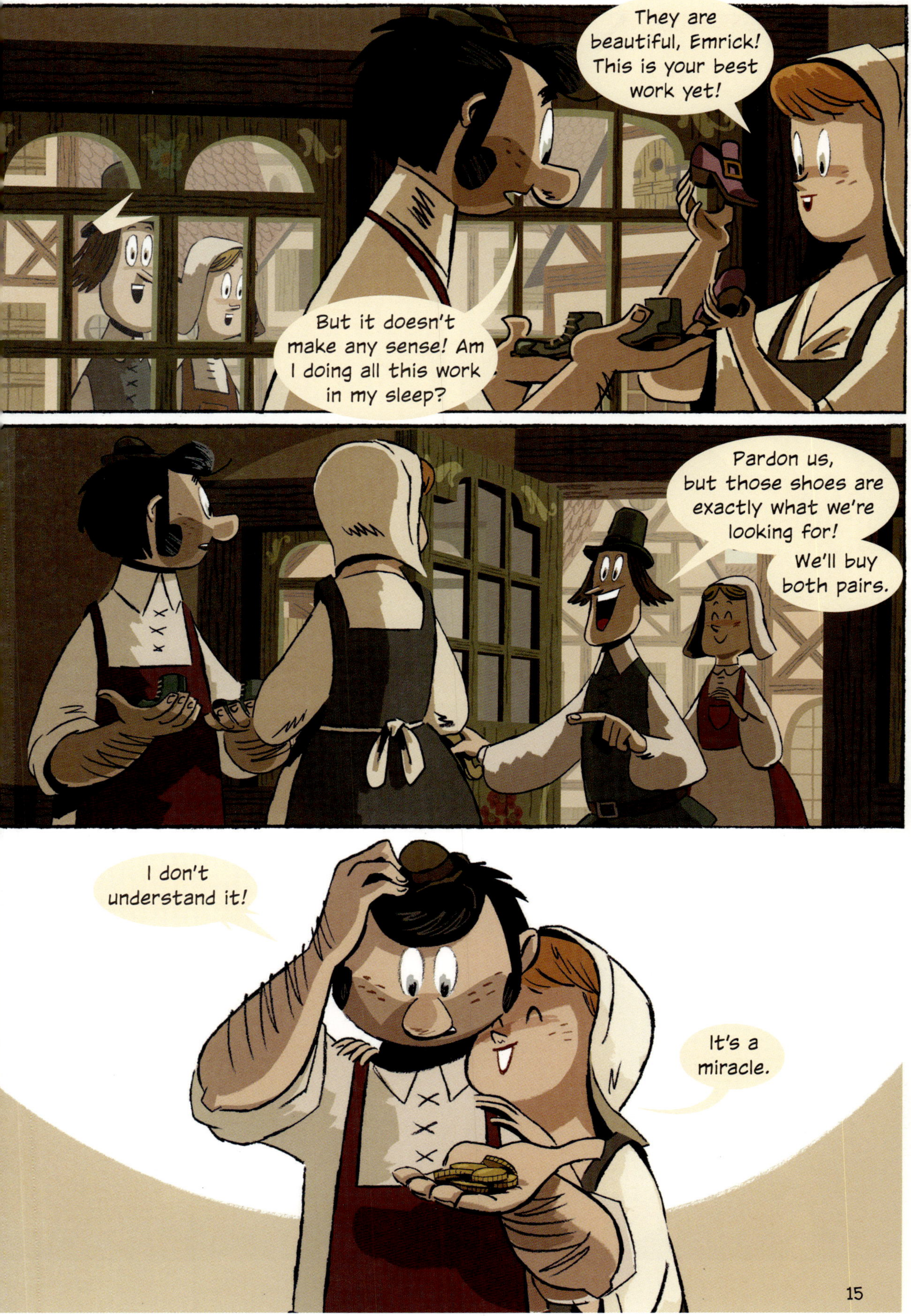
They are beautiful, Emrick! This is your best work yet!
But it doesn't make any sense! Am I doing all this work in my sleep?
Pardon us, but those shoes are exactly what we're looking for!
We'll buy both pairs.
I don't understand it!
It's a miracle.

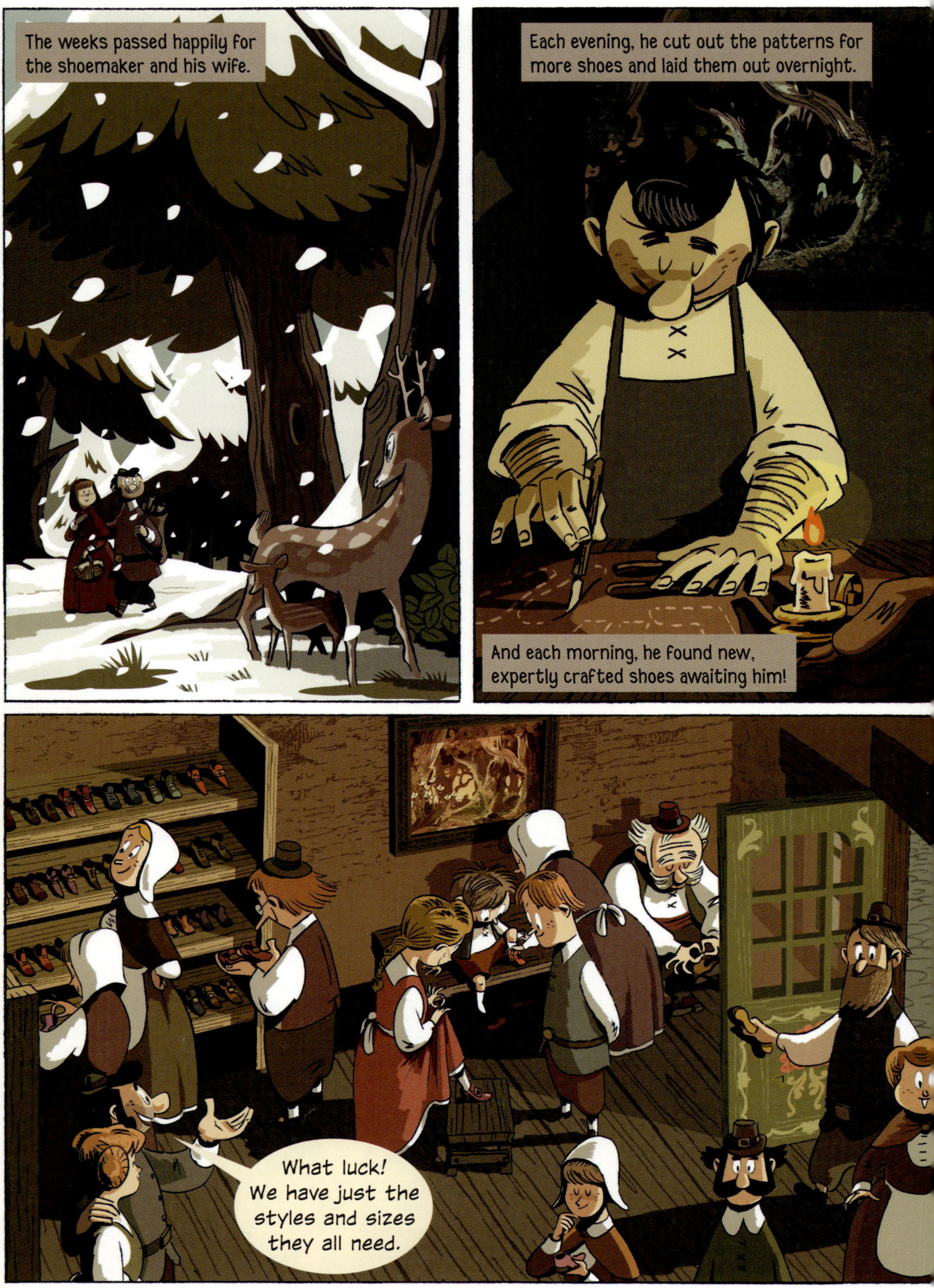
The weeks passed happily for the shoemaker and his wife.
Each evening, he cut out the patterns for more shoes and laid them out overnight.
And each morning, he found new, expertly crafted shoes awaiting him!
What luck! We have just the styles and sizes they all need.

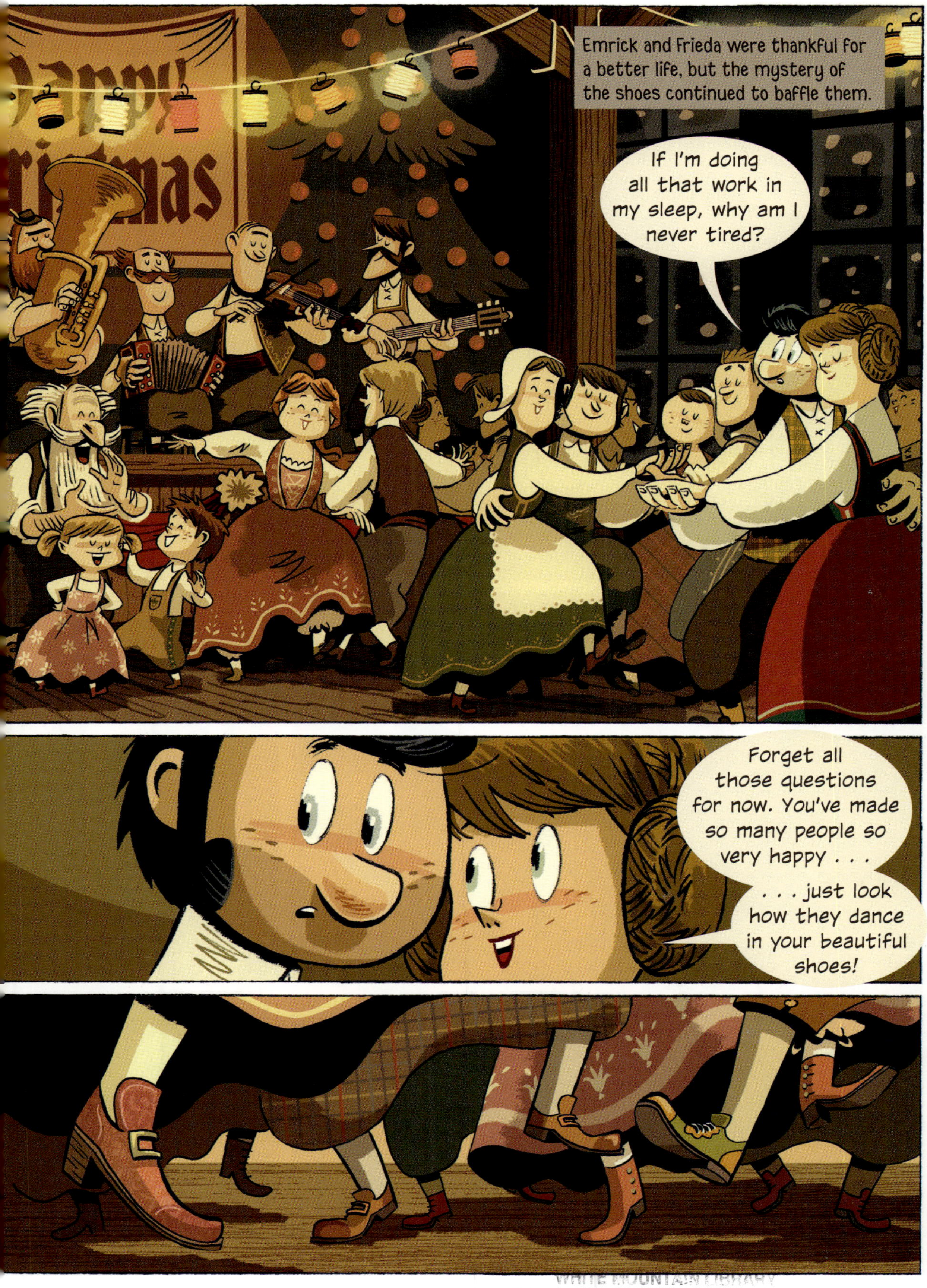
Happy Christmas
Emrick and Frieda were thankful for a better life, but the mystery of the shoes continued to baffle them.
If I'm doing all that work in my sleep, why am I never tired?
Forget all those questions for now. You've made so many people so very happy . . .
. . . just look how they dance in your beautiful shoes!

Later that night . . .
Still, I can't help but wonder how the shoes are being made.
Then let's stay awake tonight and see for ourselves!
Soon, midnight approached.
I'll leave the cut out patterns here, as usual.
This looks like a good place to hide . . .

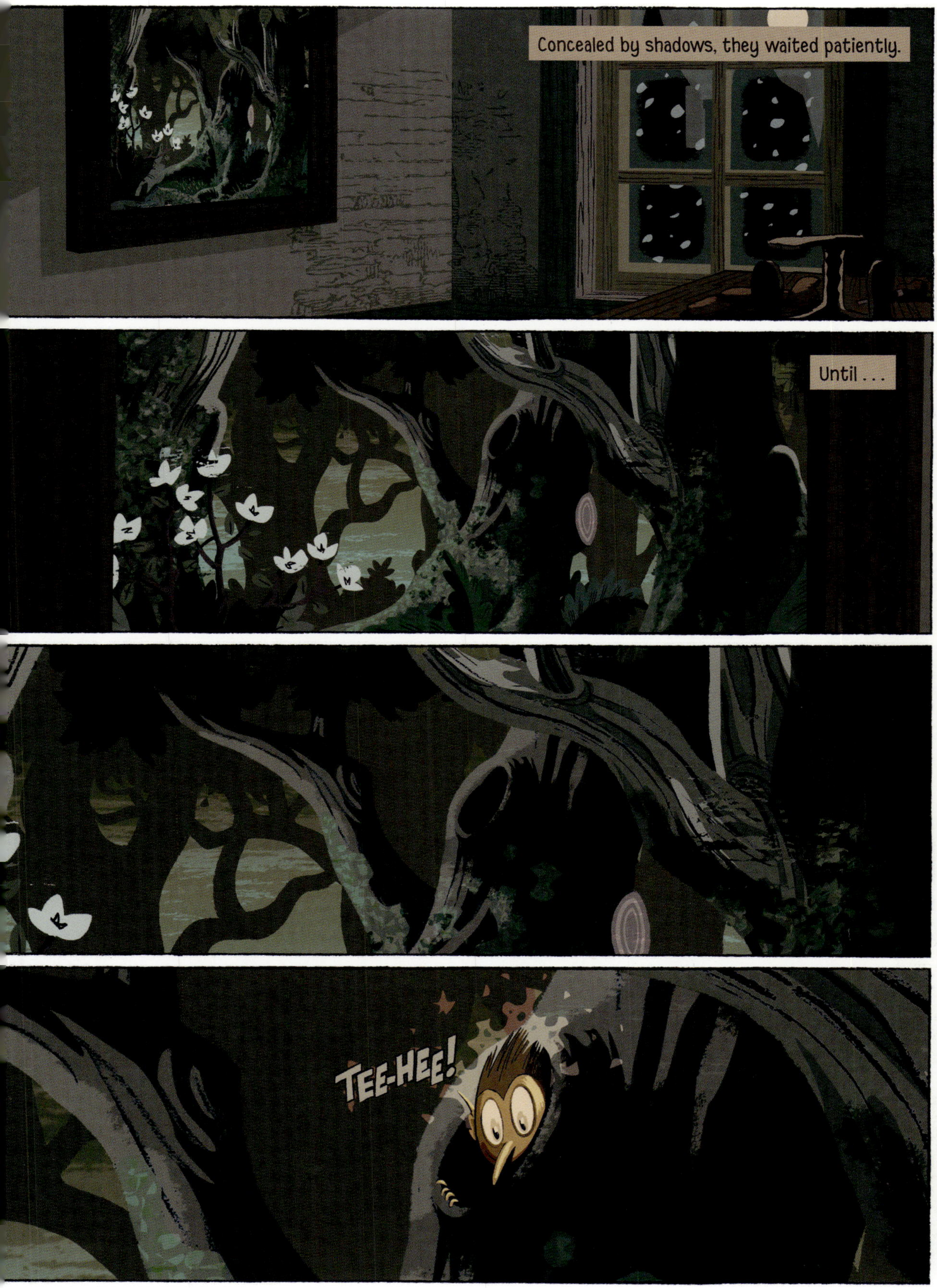
Concealed by shadows, they waited patiently.
Until . . .
TEE-HEE!

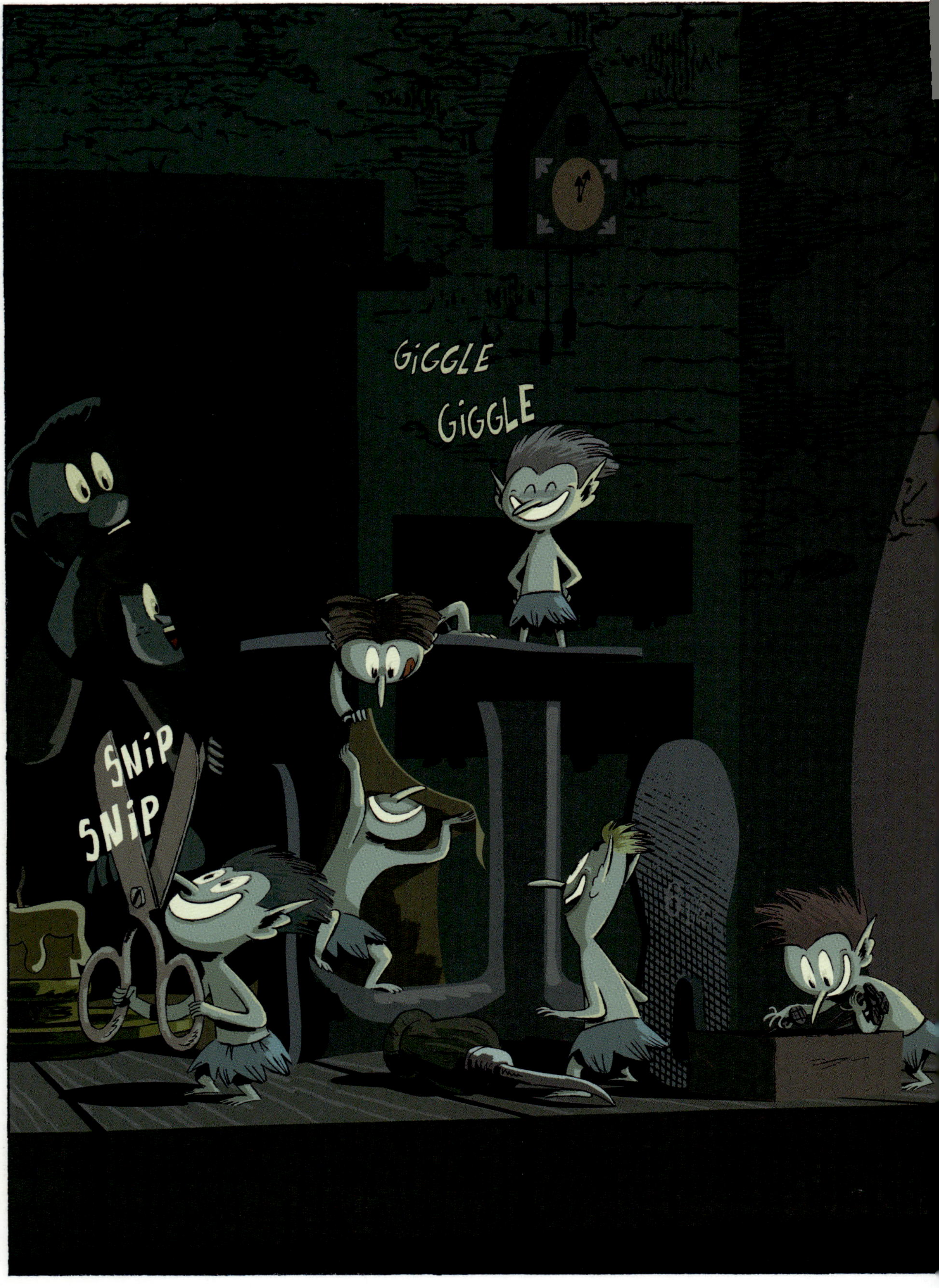
GIGGLE
GIGGLE
SNIP
SNIP

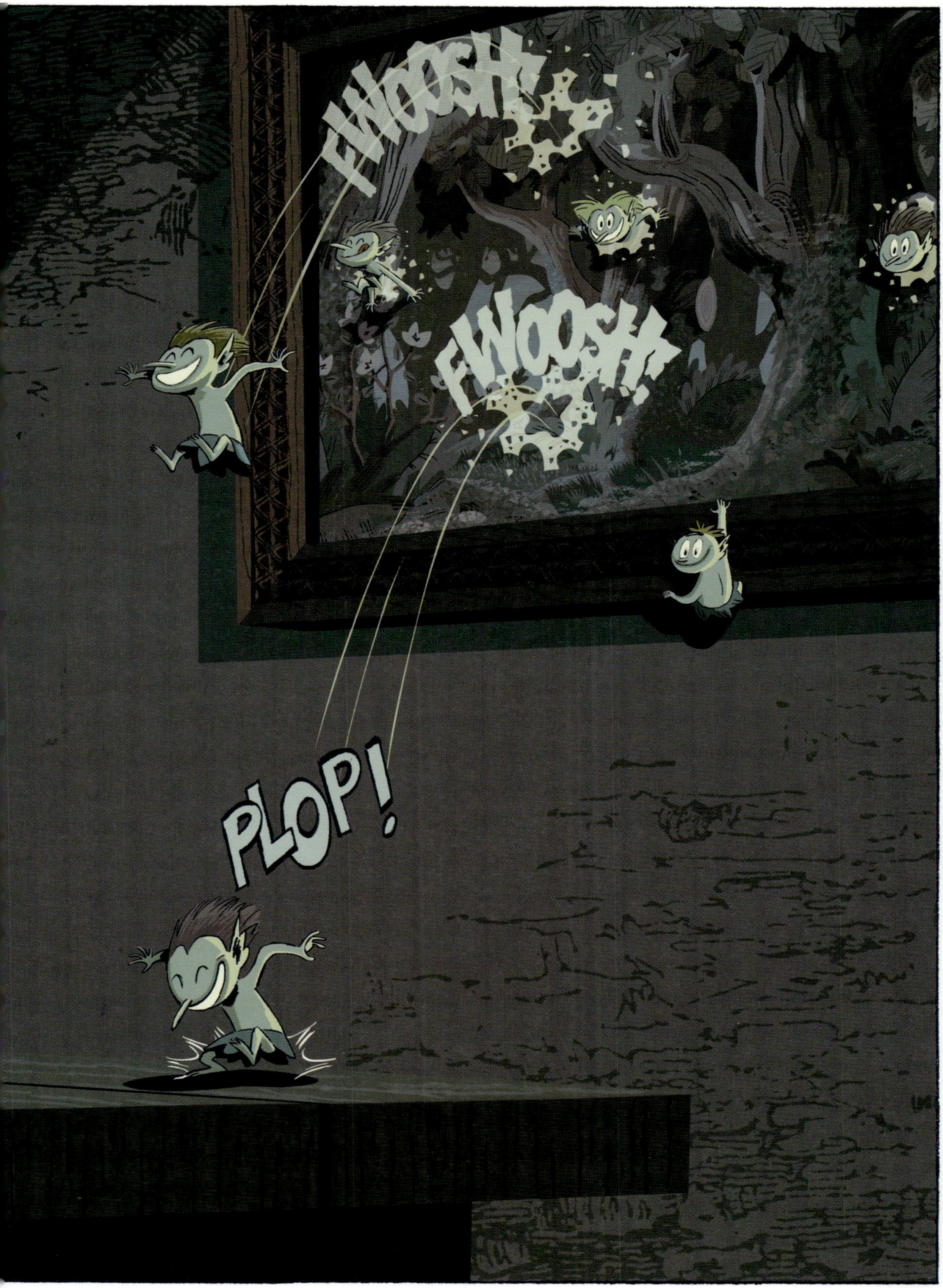
FWOOSH!
FWOOSH!
PLOP!

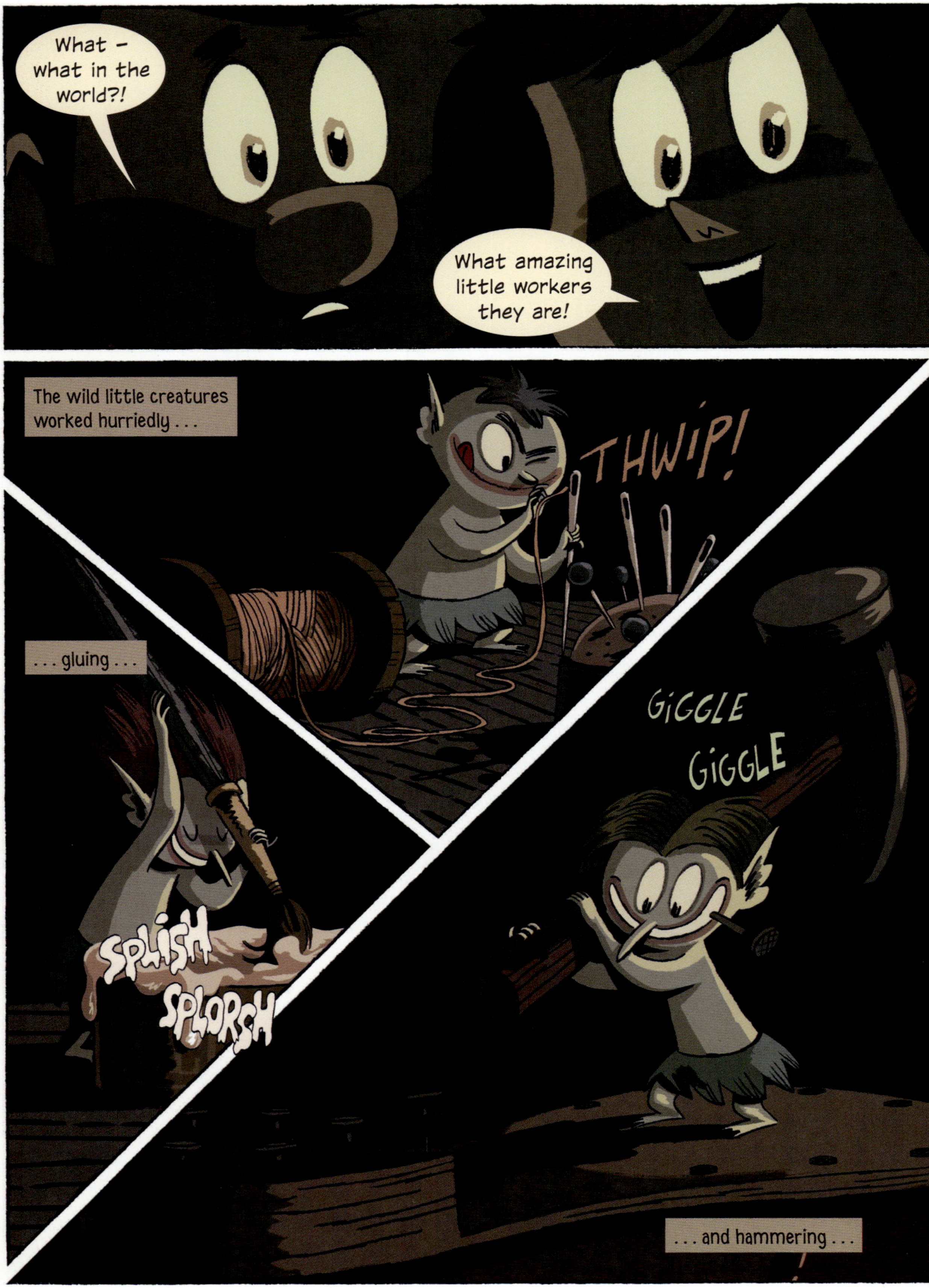
What -
what in the
world?!
What amazing
little workers
they are!
The wild little creatures
worked hurriedly . . .
THWIP!
. . . gluing . . .
SPLISH
SPLORSH
GIGGLE
GIGGLE
. . . and hammering . . .

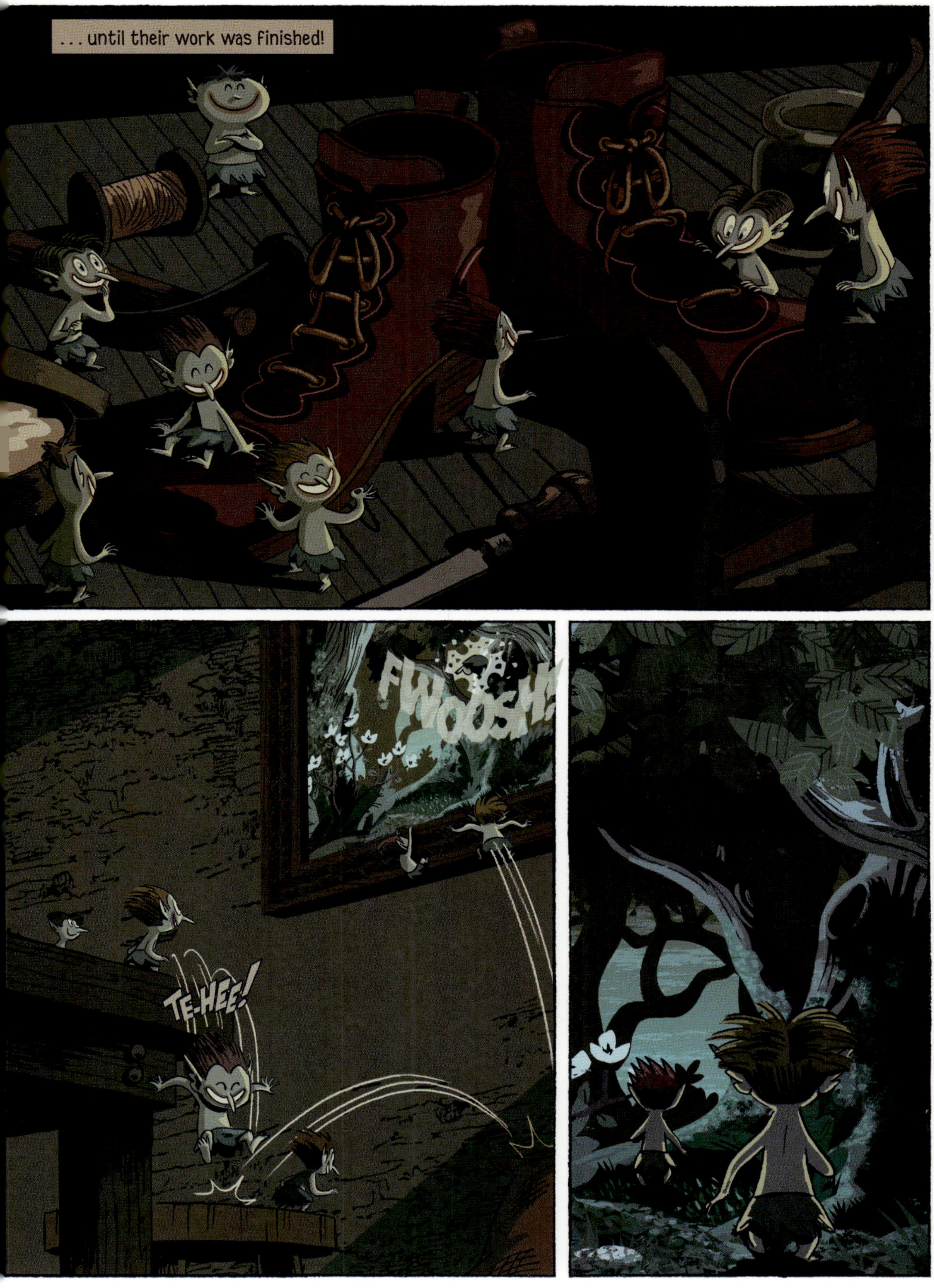

. . . until their work was finished!
FWOOSH!
TE-HEE!

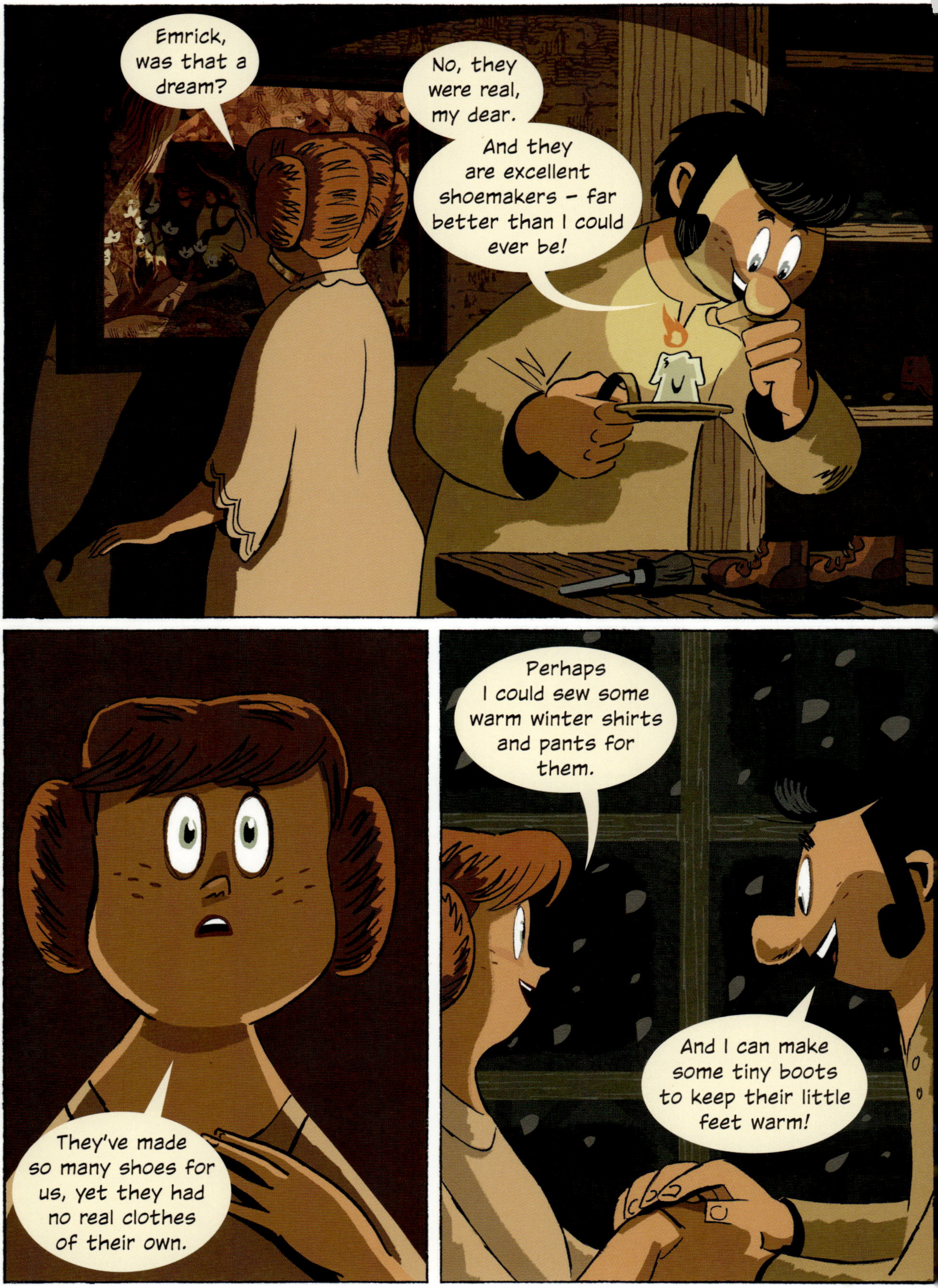
Emrick, was that a dream?
No, they were real, my dear.
And they are excellent shoemakers – far better than I could ever be!
They've made so many shoes for us, yet they had no real clothes of their own.
Perhaps I could sew some warm winter shirts and pants for them.
And I can make some tiny boots to keep their little feet warm!

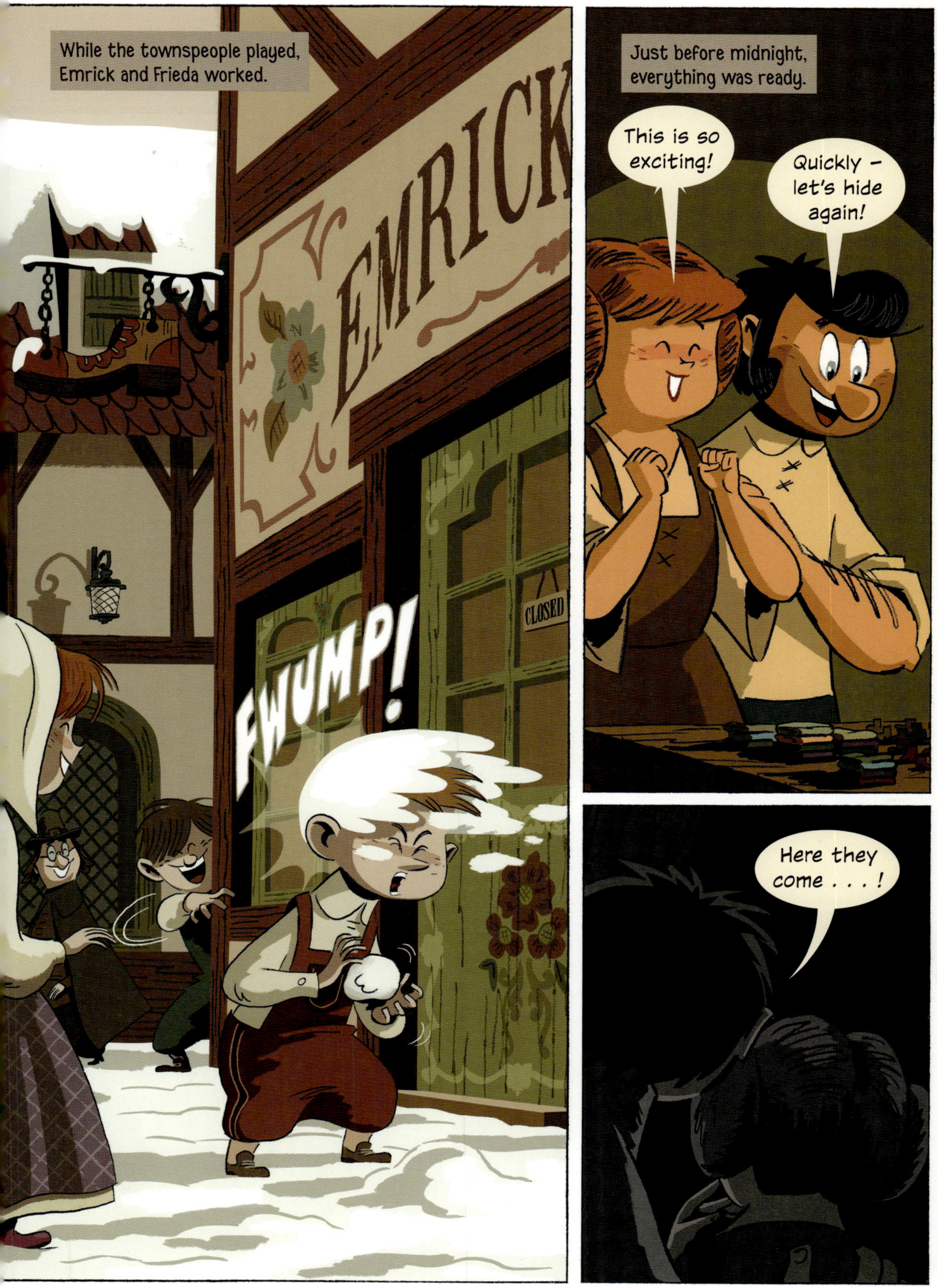
While the townspeople played, Emrick and Frieda worked.
EMRICK
CLOSED
FWUMP!
Just before midnight, everything was ready.
This is so exciting!
Quickly – let's hide again!
Here they come . . . !

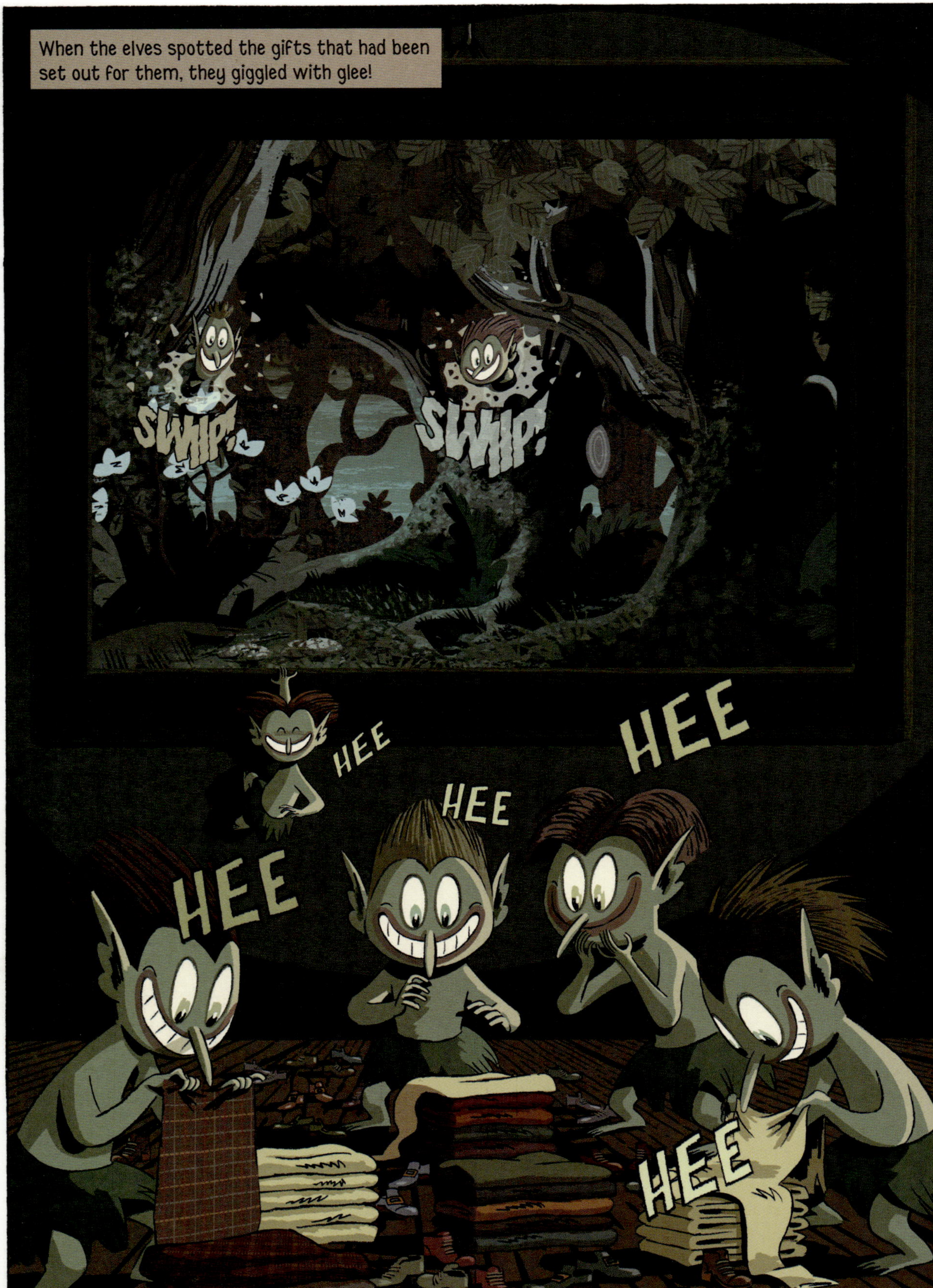
When the elves spotted the gifts that had been set out for them, they giggled with glee!
SWIP!
SWIP!
HEE
HEE
HEE
HEE
HEE

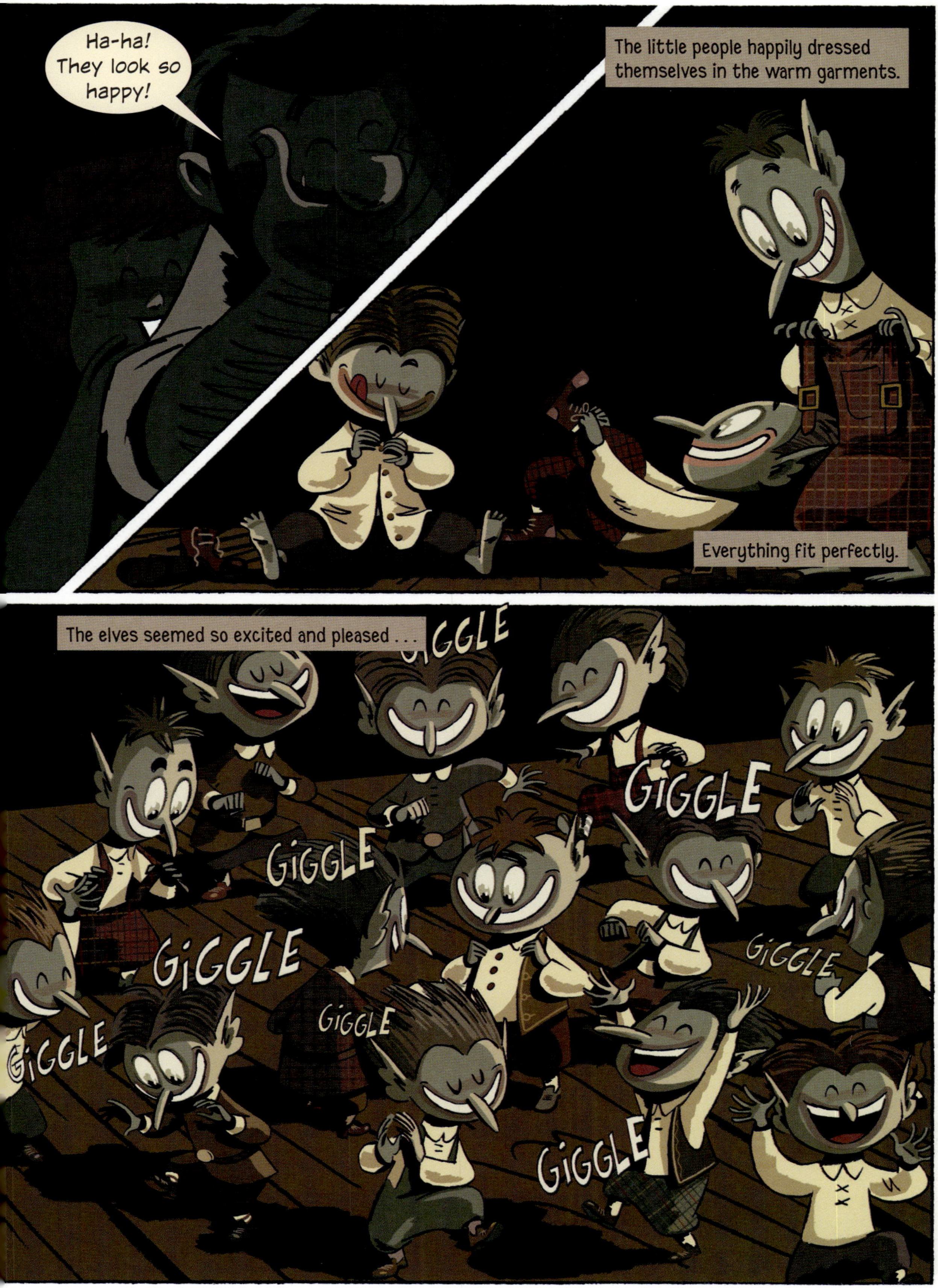
Ha-ha! They look so happy!
The little people happily dressed themselves in the warm garments.
Everything fit perfectly.
The elves seemed so excited and pleased . . .
GIGGLE
GIGGLE
GIGGLE
GIGGLE
GIGGLE
GIGGLE
GIGGLE
GIGGLE

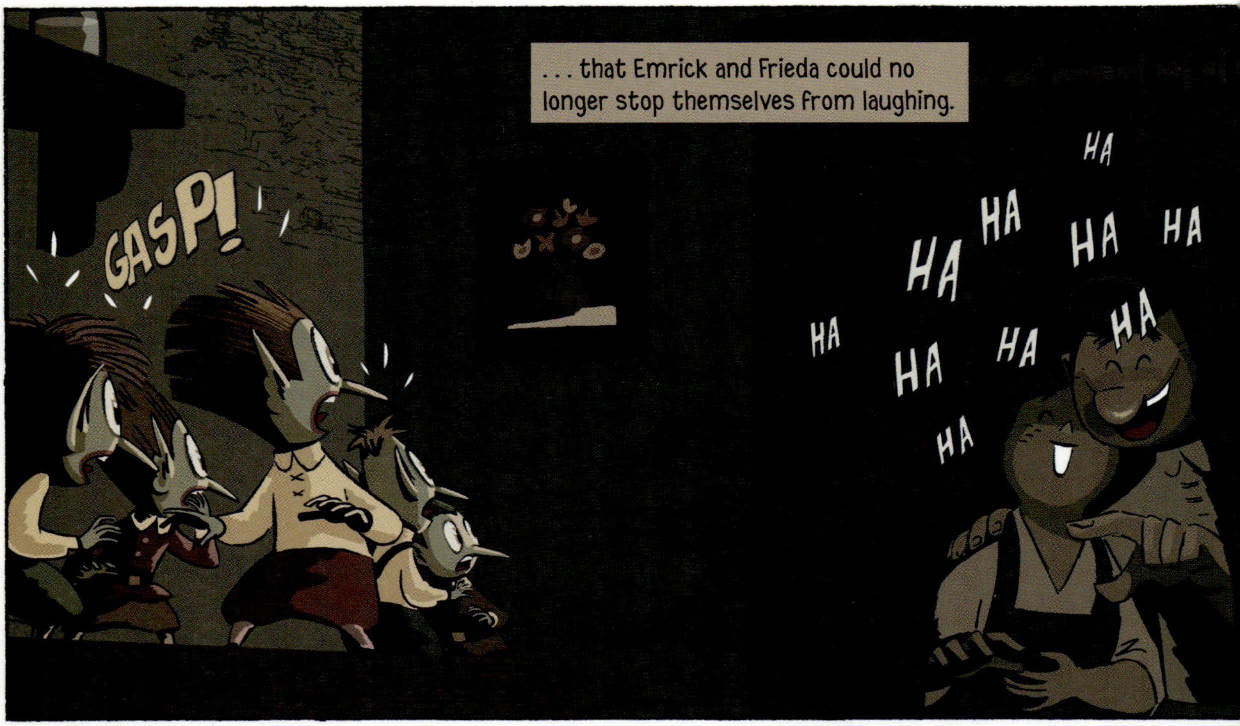
. . . that Emrick and Frieda could no longer stop themselves from laughing.
GASP!
HA HA HA HA HA HA HA HA HA HA

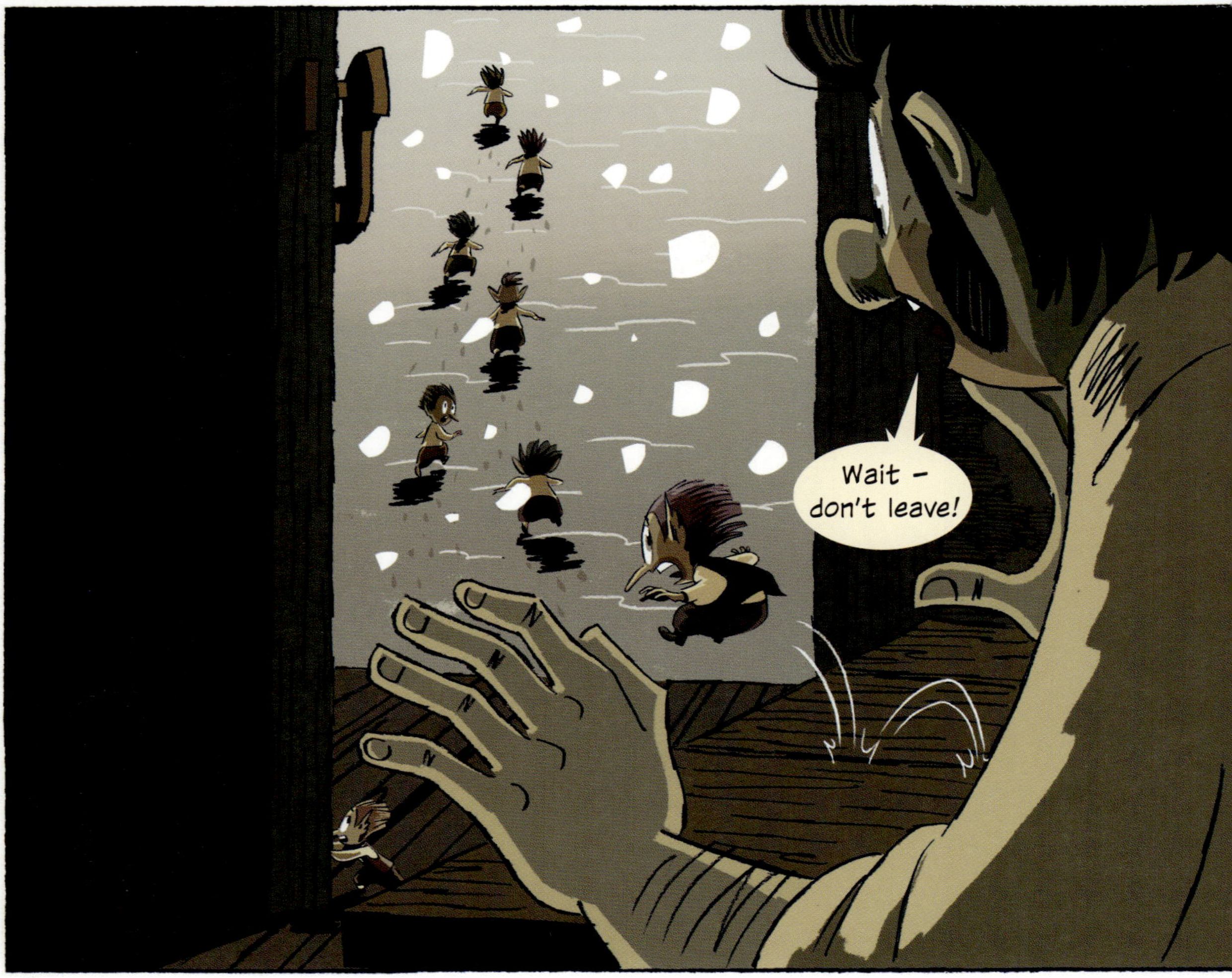
Wait - don't leave!

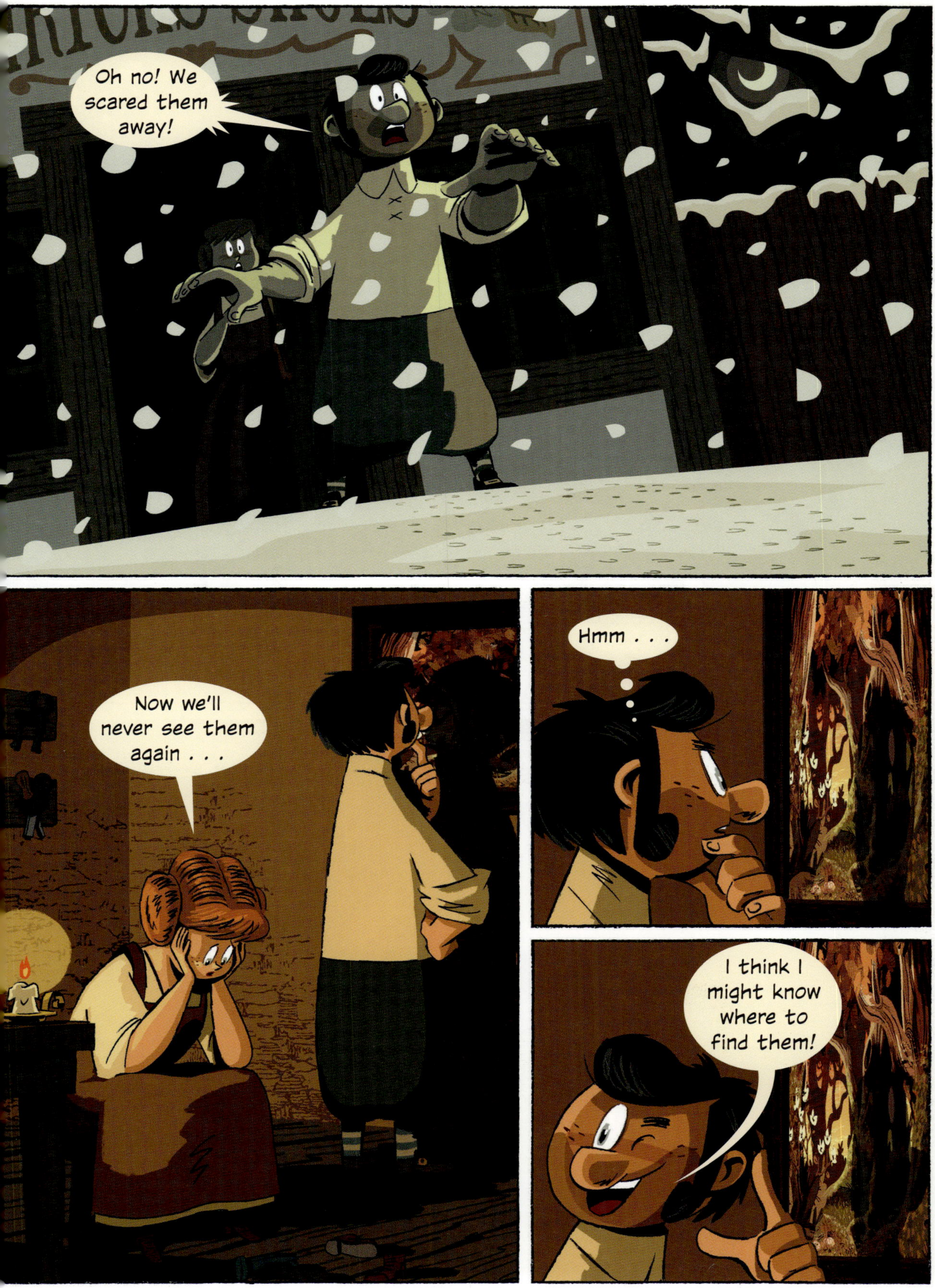
Oh no! We scared them away!
Now we'll never see them again . . .
Hmm . . .
I think I might know where to find them!

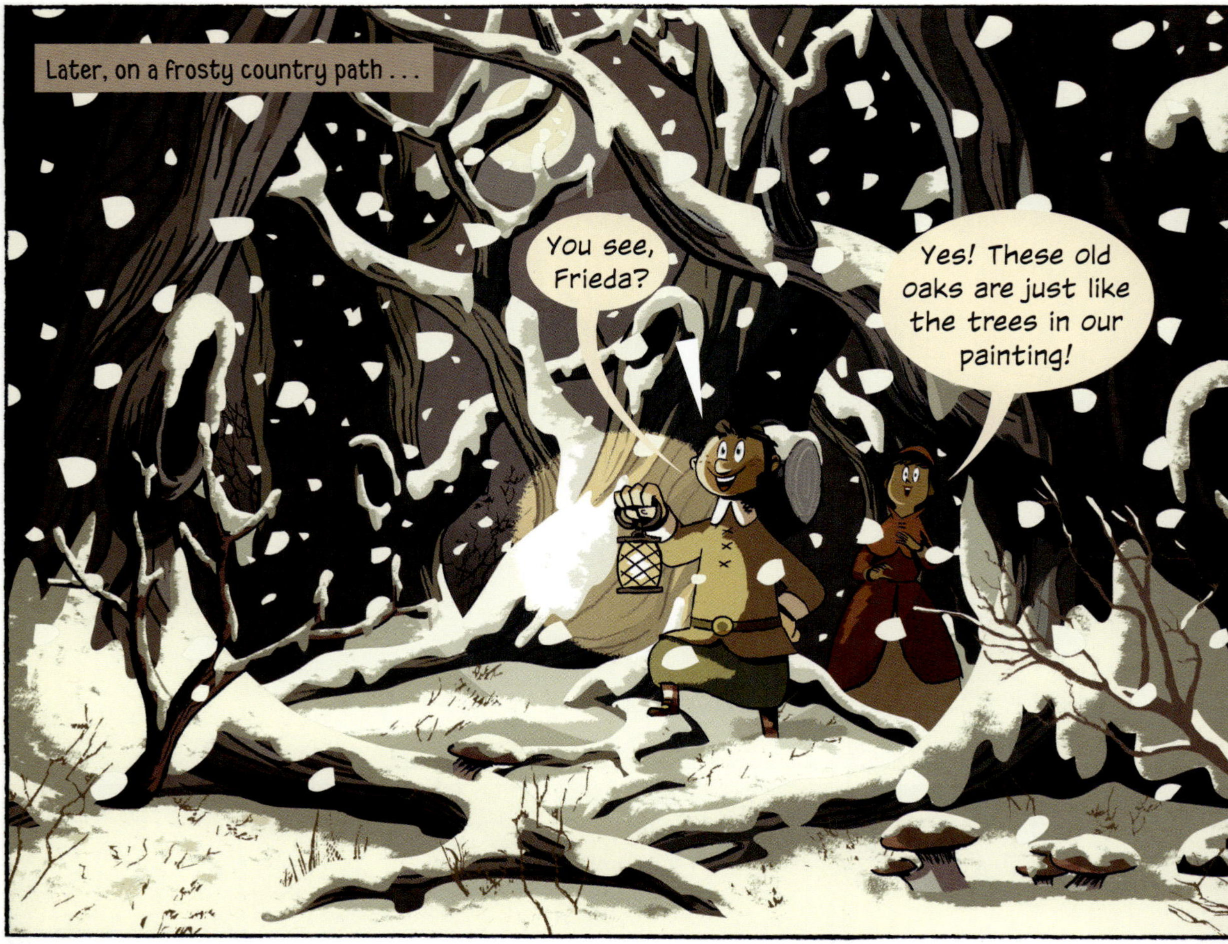
Later, on a frosty country path . . .
You see, Frieda?
Yes! These old oaks are just like the trees in our painting!

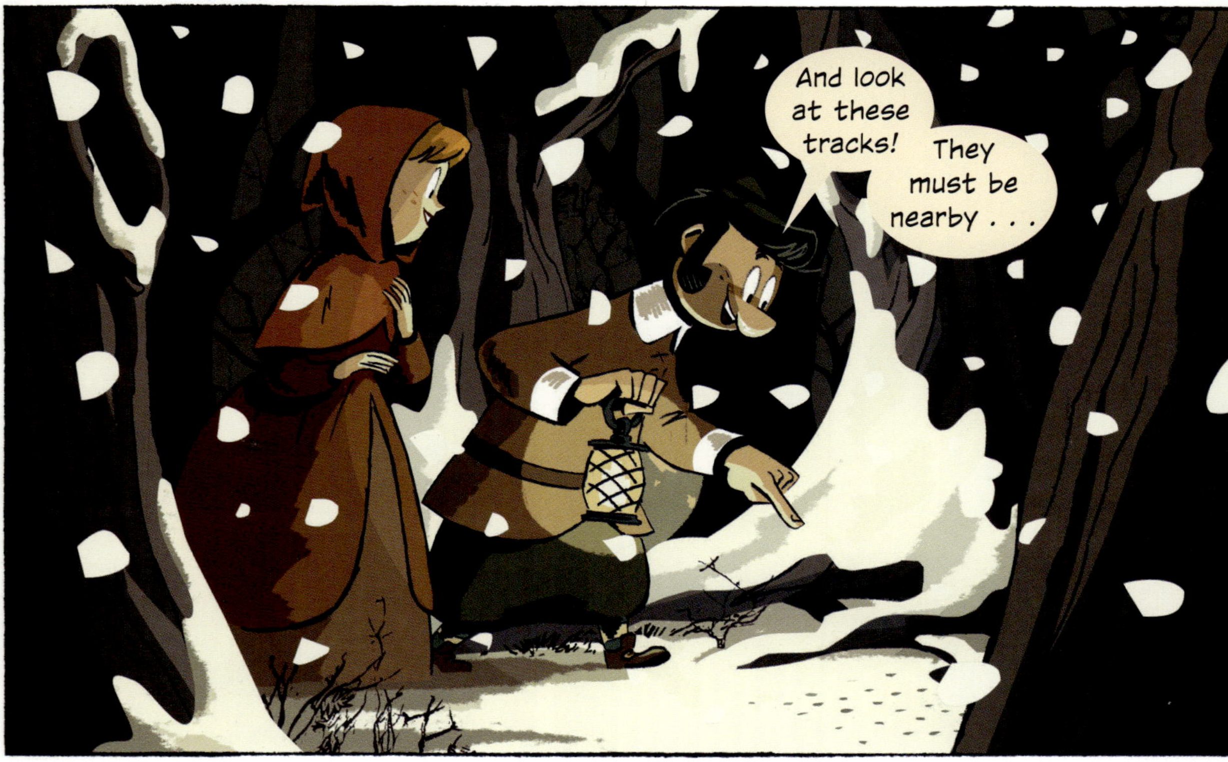
And look at these tracks!
They must be nearby . . .

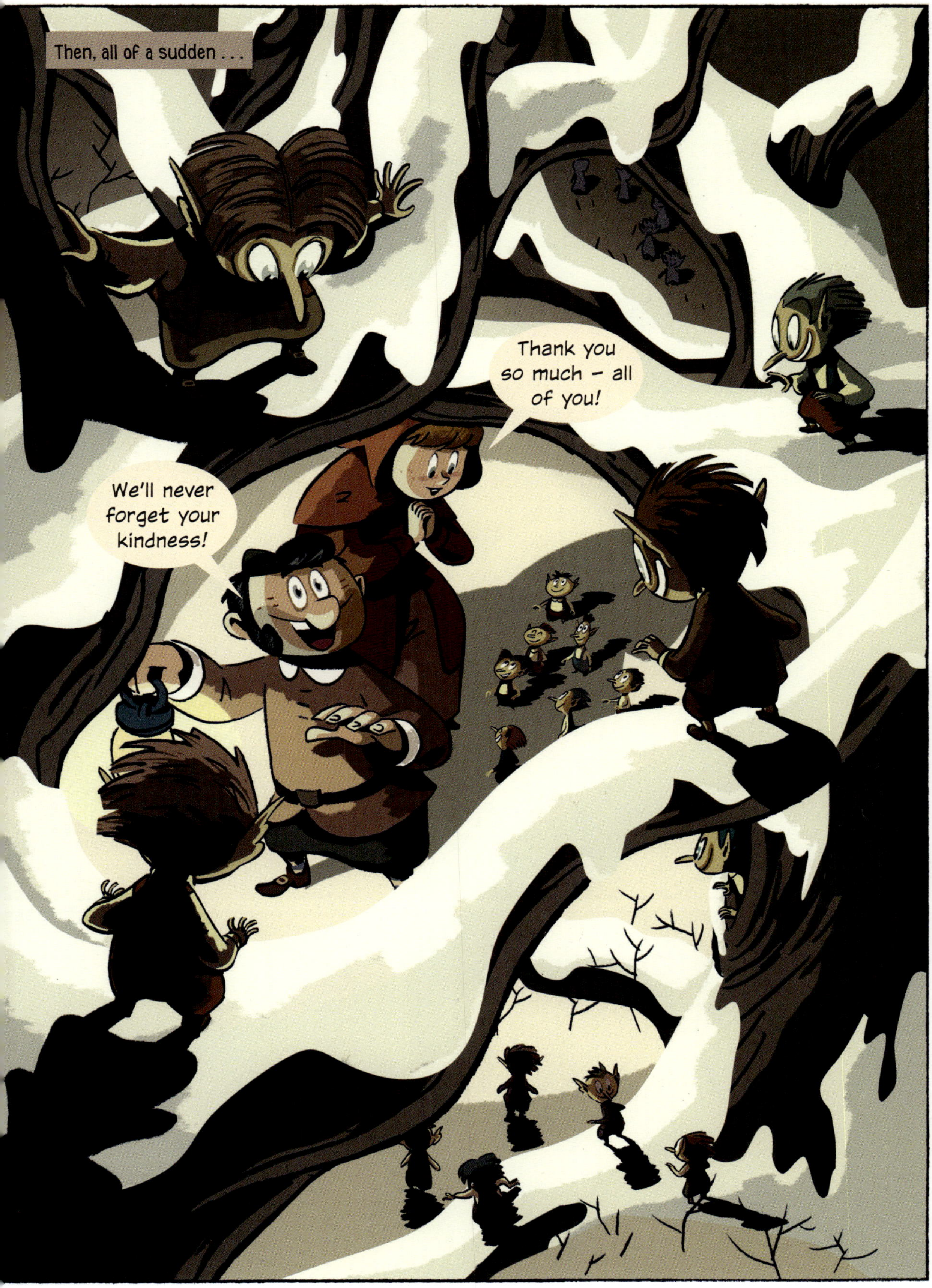
Then, all of a sudden . . .
Thank you so much – all of you!
We'll never forget your kindness!

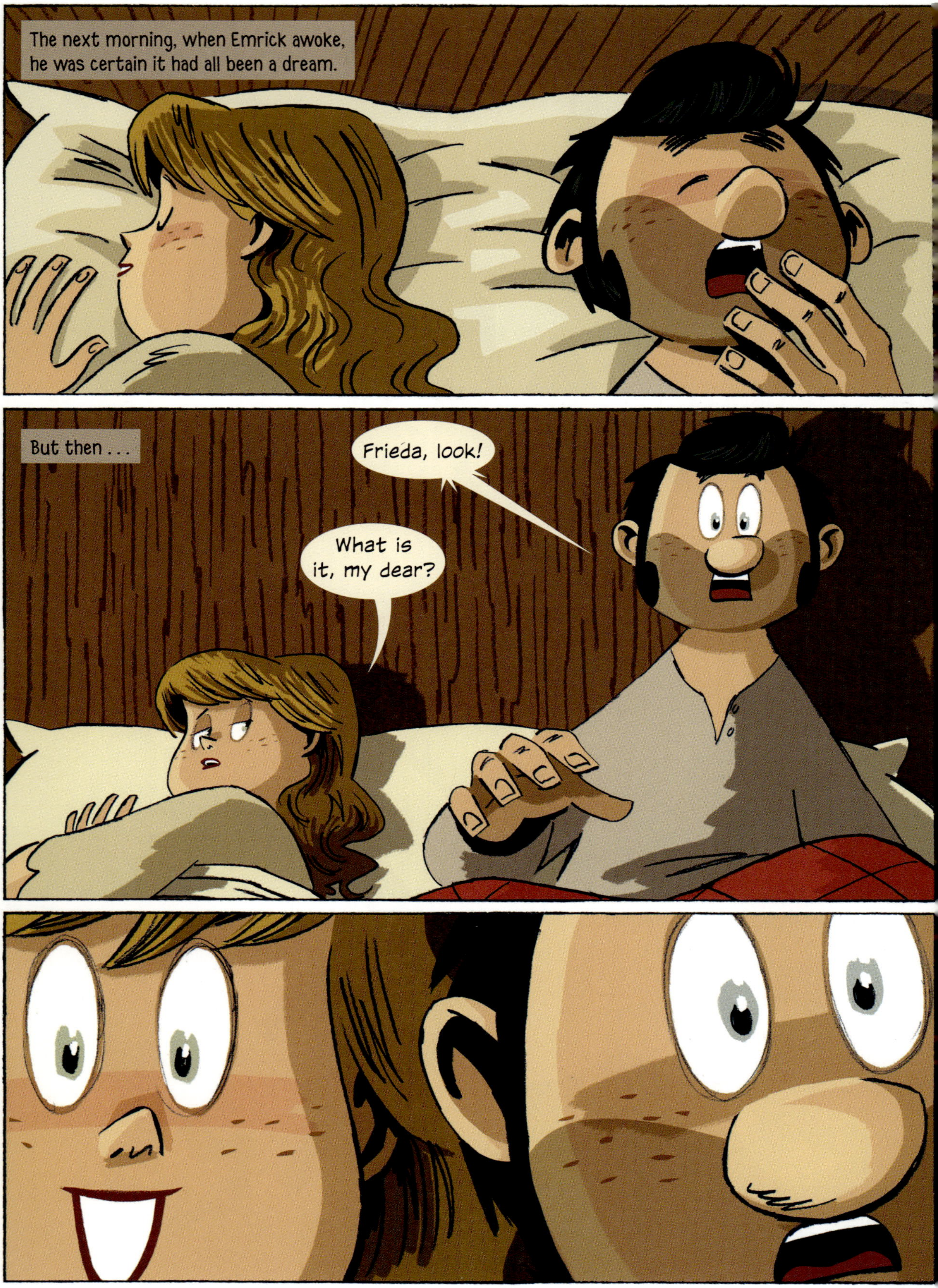
The next morning, when Emrick awoke, he was certain it had all been a dream.
But then . . .
Frieda, look!
What is it, my dear?

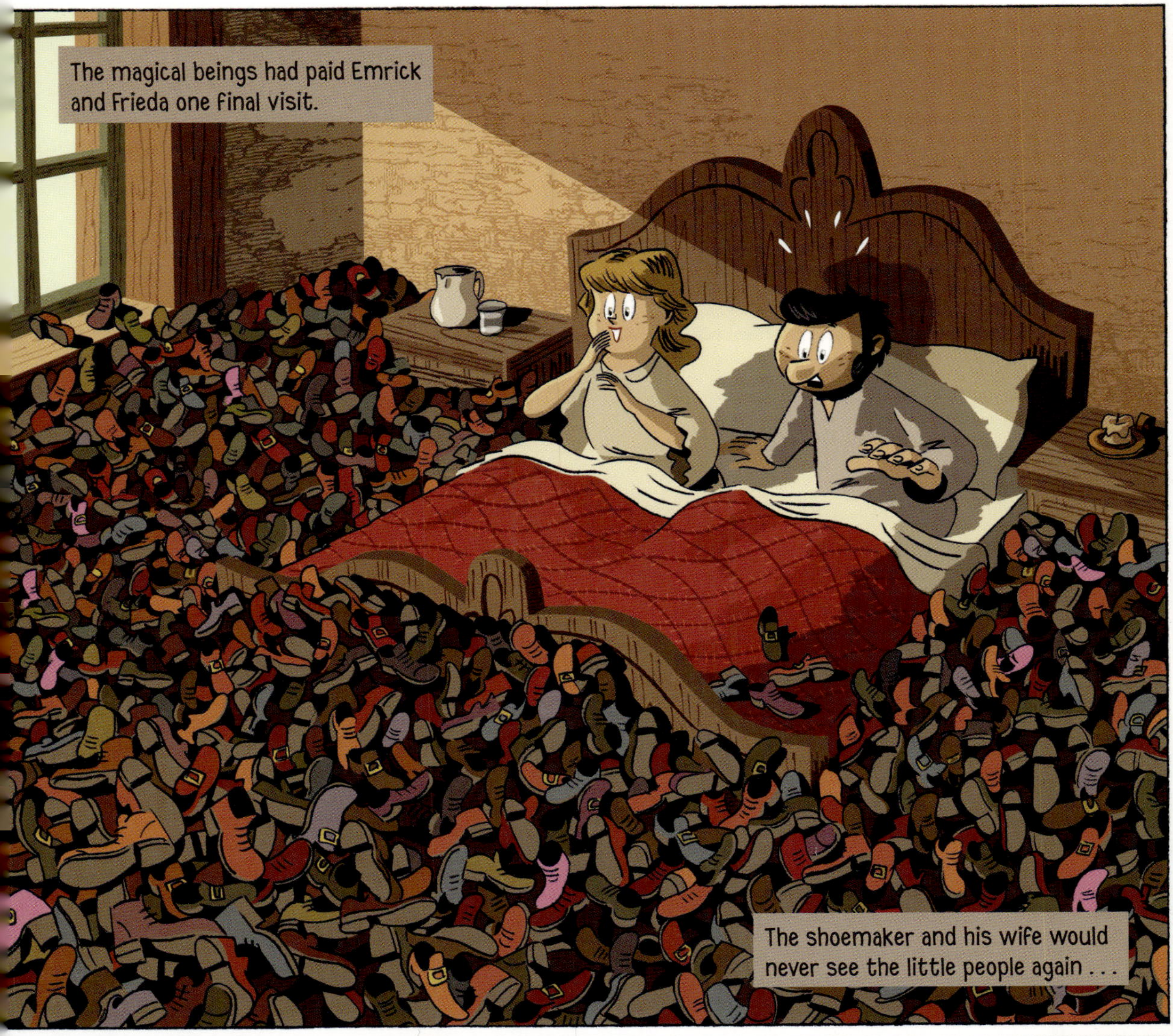
The magical beings had paid Emrick and Frieda one final visit.
The shoemaker and his wife would never see the little people again . . .

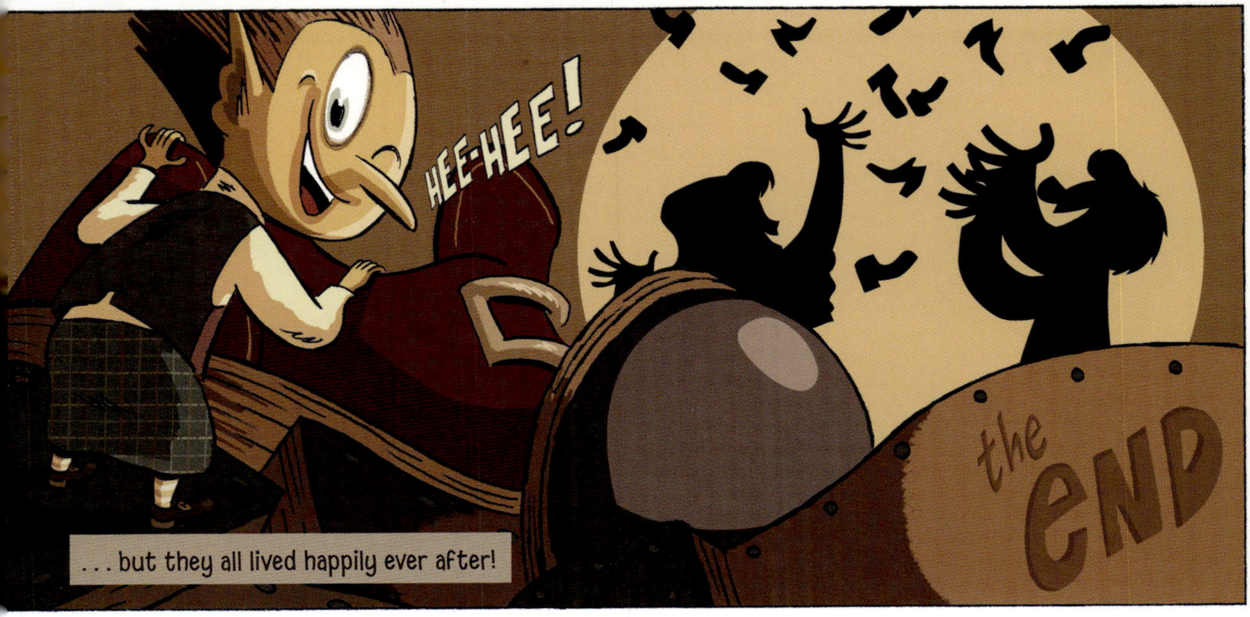
HEE-HEE!
. . . but they all lived happily ever after!
the END

The Brothers Grimm

A FAMILY OF FOLK AND FAIRY TALES

Jacob and Wilhelm Grimm were German brothers who invited storytellers to their home so they could write down their tales.

Peasants and villagers, middle-class citizens, wealthy aristocrats — even the Grimms' servants — contributed to their diverse collection of stories!

The brothers also collected folk tales from published works from other cultures and languages, adding to the variety of their sources.

In 1812, the Grimms published their collection of fairy tales, called *Children's and Household Tales.* The Brothers Grimm were among the first to collect and publish folk and fairy tales taken directly from the people who told them. These days, it would be hard to find anyone who hasn't at least heard of one of the Grimm Brothers' colorful characters!

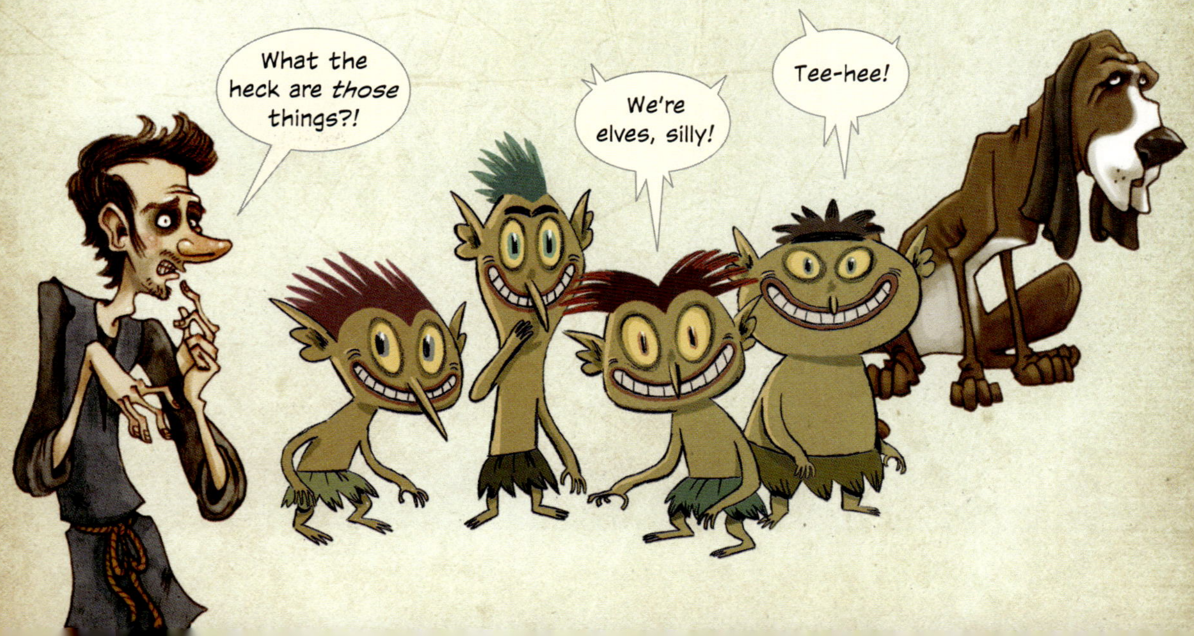
What the heck are *those* things?!
We're elves, silly!
Tee-hee!

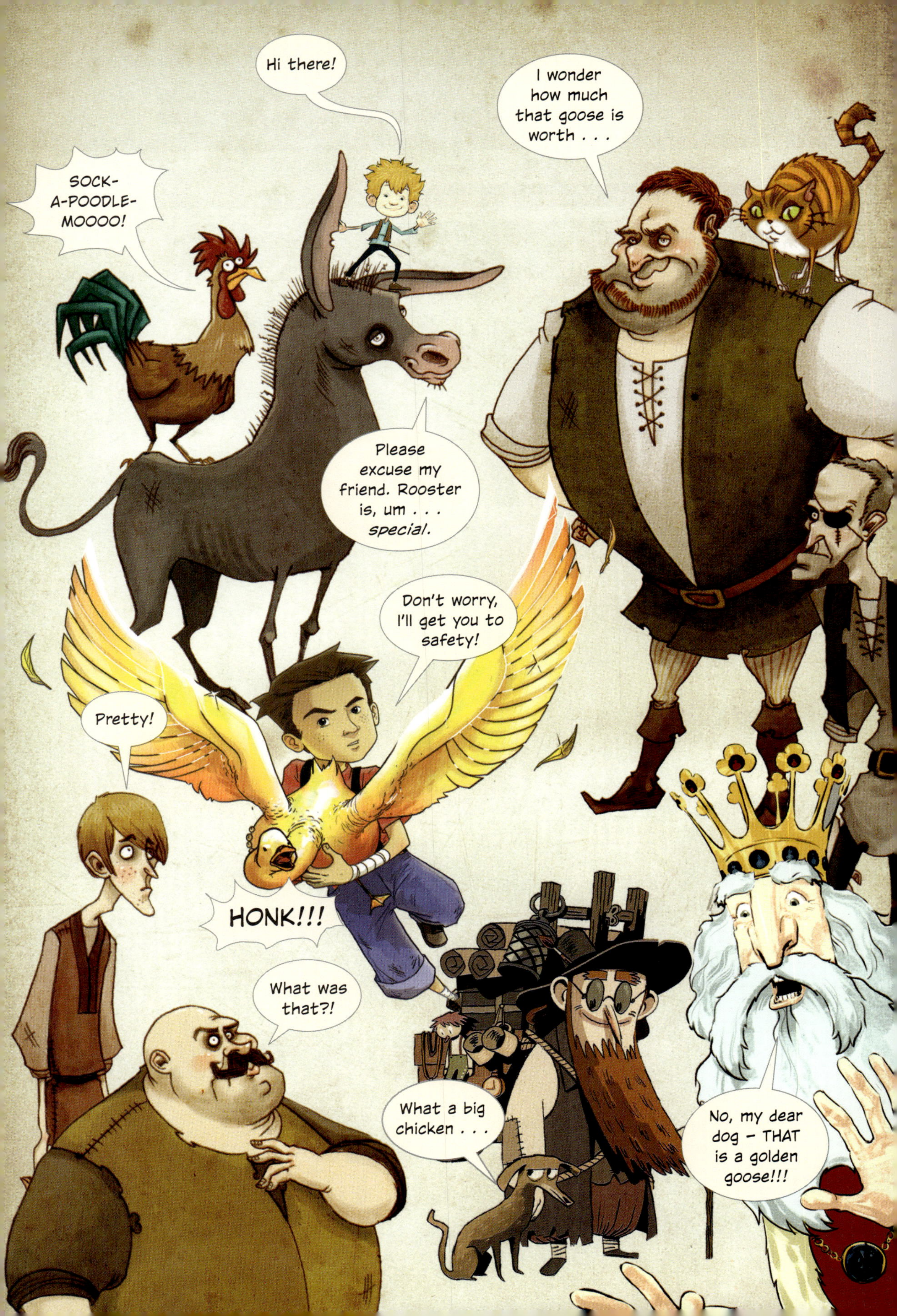
Hi there!
I wonder how much that goose is worth . . .
SOCK-A-POODLE-MOOOO!
Please excuse my friend. Rooster is, um . . . *special*.
Don't worry, I'll get you to safety!
Pretty!
HONK!!!
What was that?!
What a big chicken . . .
No, my dear dog – THAT is a golden goose!!!

STONE ARCH BOOKS PRESENTS ANOTHER

Grimm Graphic Novel . . .

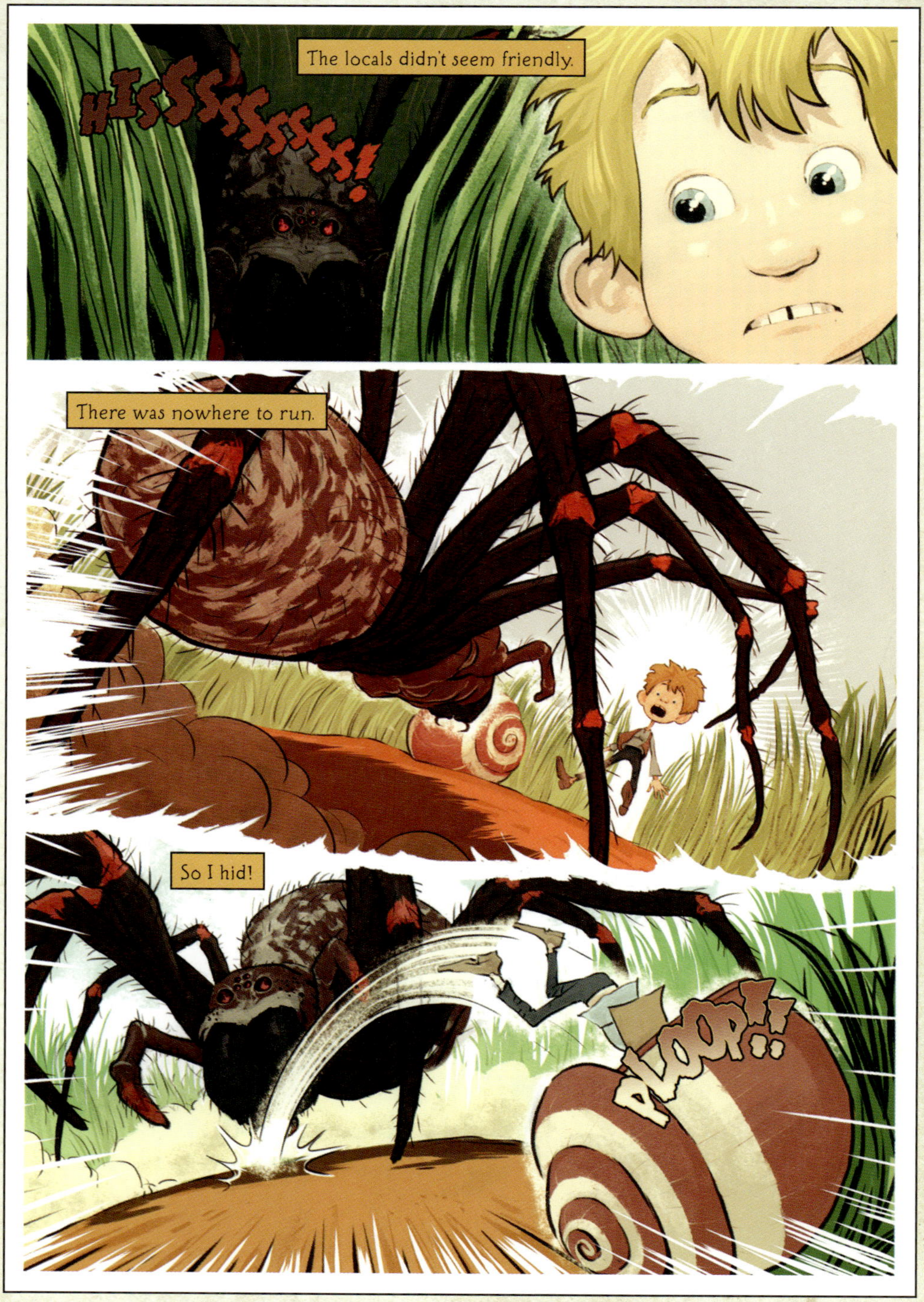

The locals didn't seem friendly.
HISSSSSSSSS!
There was nowhere to run.
So I hid!
PLOOP!!

Read Tom Thumb

ONLY FROM STONE ARCH BOOKS!

About the Retelling Author

Martin Powell has been a freelance writer since 1986. He has written hundreds of stories, many of which have been published by Disney, Marvel, Tekno comix, Moonstone Books, and others. In 1989, Powell received an Eisner Award nomination for his graphic novel *Scarlet in Gaslight*. This award is one of the highest comic book honors.

About the Illustrator

Pedro Rodriquez studied illustration at the Fine Arts School in Barcelona, Spain. He has worked in design, marketing, and advertising, creating books, logos, animated films, and music videos. Rodriquez lives in Barcelona with his wife, Gemma, and their daughter Maya.

Discussion Questions

1. Emrick and Frieda thank the elves for their help by making them some clothing. What's the best gift you've ever received? Talk about your presents.

2. Which illustration in this book is your favorite? Why?

3. Emrick is a talented shoemaker. What are your talents? Talk about your skills and abilities.

Writing Prompts

1. Emrick's trade, or job, is shoemaking. If you could pick any trade to do for a living, what would you choose? Write about your new career.

2. Emrick was a generous person. In what ways have you been generous? Write about the nice things you've done for other people.

3. The elves emerged from inside a magic painting. Why do you think they helped Emrick and Frieda? Write a story from the elves' point of view that explains who they are, where they come from, and what they want.

Glossary

BAFFLE (BAF-uhl) — to puzzle or confuse someone

CONCEALED (kuhn-SEELD) — hid

CRAFT (KRAFT) — work or a hobby in which you make things with your hands

ERRAND (AIR-uhnd) — a short or quick trip to get something done

FINEST (FINE-est) — the best, or the most elegant

GARMENT (GAR-muhnt) — piece of clothing

GENEROSITY (jen-er-OSS-i-tee) — people who are generous are happy to use their time and money to help others

INSISTED (in-SIST-id) — demanded something very firmly

MIRACLE (MEER-uh-kuhl) — an amazing event that cannot be explained by the laws of nature

PEDDLER (PED-uhl-ur) — someone who travels around and sells things

STRANGE (STRAYNJ) — different from the usual, odd, or unfamiliar

SUITED (SOOT-id) — was acceptable and convenient

More

Grimm Brothers GRAPHIC NOVELS

by STONE ARCH BOOKS . . .

A GRIMM GRAPHIC NOVEL
THE BREMEN TOWN MUSICIANS
retold by Louise Simonson
illustrated by Lisa Weber

A GRIMM GRAPHIC NOVEL
The Golden Goose
retold by Sean Tulien
illustrated by Thiago Ferras

A GRIMM GRAPHIC NOVEL
TOM THUMB

STILL WANT MORE?

Find cool websites and more books like this one at www.Facthound.com.

Just type in the Book ID: **9781434225535** and you're ready to go!

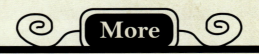

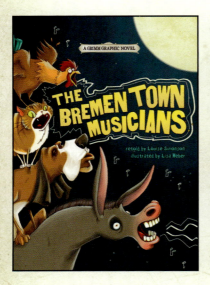

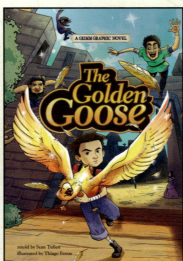

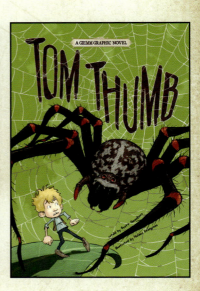